Prodigies

Prodigies

a novel

Angélica Gorodischer

Translated by Sue Burke

Small Beer Press
Easthampton, MA

Prodigios
© Angélica Gorodischer, 1994

Prodigios copyright © 1994 by Angélica Gorodischer. All rights reserved.
Translation copyright © 2015 by Sue Burke. All rights reserved.
Cover illustration © 2015 by Elisabeth Alba. All rights reserved. (albaillustration.com)

Small Beer Press
150 Pleasant Street #306
Easthampton, MA 01027
smallbeerpress.com
weightlessbooks.com
info@smallbeerpress.com

Distributed to the trade by Consortium.

Library of Congress Cataloging-in-Publication Data

Gorodischer, Angélica.
[Prodigios. English]
Prodigies : a novel / Angélica Gorodischer ; translated by Sue Burke. -- First edition.
     pages cm
     Summary: "An enchanting incantatory novel of the women whose lives pass through a
nineteenth century boarding house. Moving, subtle, and dreamlike"-- Provided by publisher.
     ISBN 978-1-61873-099-2 (paperback) -- ISBN 978-1-61873-100-5 (ebook)
     1. Women--Germany--Fiction. 2. Boardinghouses--Germany--Fiction. 3. Germany--Histo-
ry--1789-1900--Fiction. I. Burke, Sue, 1955- translator. II. Title.
     PQ7798.17.O73P7613 2015
     863'.64--dc23
                              2015010357

First edition 1 2 3 4 5 6 7 8 9

Text set in Centaur MT.

Printed on 50# 30% PCR recycled Natures Natural paper by the Maple Press in York, PA.

This book is for my friends

Chita Luraschi
Hebe Caviglia
María del Carmen Marini
Maria Ester Paoletti
Mele Bruniard
Nidia Armengod
Susana Paoletti
Tatá Raimondi
Verónica Lardone

and for my northern sisters

Marie Nimier
Ursula K. Le Guin

. . . for things truly begin
behind the things that happen.

— João Guimarães Rosa

Part One: Illusion

Part Two: Toni Plays

Part Three: Prodigies

Part One: Illusion

I. Nothing Will Be As It Was

On the day Madame Nashiru arrived at the boarding house on Scheller Street, a brief tremor passed through the house, unnoticed by everyone except Katja. The foundations of the world did not shudder, plagues did not break out, first-born did not die, there were no catastrophes, the waters of the Genil River did not inundate a dozen towns, black death did not arrive at Addis Ababa, the sorcerers of Yauyuos did not dream about dogs with human heads, the walls of Nerja Cave did not crack, ships did not sink in the inlets of Baffin, volcanoes did not erupt, islands did not disappear, orchards did not suffer drought, the lintels of old cathedrals did not become besooted, cemetery guards did not worry needlessly, nor did police officers or transportation inspectors or sergeants or jailors or tax collectors or judges or executioners; but the house shook, and Katja, who was in the courtyard bending over a tin-plate pan, looked at the water and told herself that there are beings with wings and yet they hide them. She did not know what she meant by that, but she was used to those sudden obscure thoughts, so she was not frightened and did not stop what she was doing to stand still and think about what it might be, what it might mean, why she had thought it, if it was a memory, something she had heard in passing, whatever it was. She already knew how, silently and unsurprised, to tell herself things that seemed meant for someone else and perhaps they were, whose meaning escaped her like a fairy, like a fearful little animal that might also have wings, hidden or not, with hardened forewings that enclosed tender, weak hindwings that the wind, even the wind could rip. She let them escape, it's okay, you can go, I won't stop you, the afternoon is too beautiful, close your eyes at night and may nothing foul from mirrors or from far away trouble your mind, and don't think about it in the morning. There are beings who have wings and yet they hide them. In the pan, the water rippled as if from a puff of wind, and Katja waited; waited, rag in hand to clean the windowpanes, until they calmed. I'm not going to put a rag there—she had created and understood that thought. I'm not going to put a rag there into the winged beings between the drops in the water. She waited while Madame Helena welcomed Madame Nashiru, and the house felt suspicious, but only Katja noticed.

The wood, the soft skeleton that persists, that can burn and rise up against a backlight when only a well and a stairway into emptiness remain, the wood was what felt it the most since it had never stopped living, or fossils, coal or ashes, never: in the beams and the doorframes, in the lintels and the parapets and the banisters, in the baseboards and the parquet, in the floors and the windowsills, in the framework, in the cheap pine of the attic, the imperfect lignin fibers twisted, created a tiny space between themselves, then stretched and returned sadly to their places, searching for each other, fitting a convex curve into another's hollow, obedient. The trees the world over, they say, it has been said and affirmed again and again in towns and long ago, touch each other, every single one, with a single root that starts in a lake called Yize, runs seven miles and divides into seven roots that each divide into seventy roots and each divide into seven hundred roots and so on beneath the whole world including the seas, and they feed the trees. Katja was convinced, how could it be otherwise? And looking at the rough trunks in the park, she would try to see the network like veins, would look at her wrists and the crook of her elbow and then at the ground where she was walking. She had tried to tell Wulda what she knew; of course Wulda was stupid and understood nothing, her fingers were wool and her brain a stone, looking at her the way a dog would look at her while she was talking. Wulda's head did not quiver, but the stones in the foundations of the house did in raspy voices that became a chorus in the marble in bathrooms, kitchen, thresholds, and steps at the entrance, and in white grains of years-dry mortar that slipped from moldings. The fretwork and grilles, peaks, gutters, window catches, hinges, lightning rods and faucets, wrought iron, ceiling rosettes, chimney grates, railings, door plates and fences whined as if rust were eating them. The gables and fascia, soffits, mullions, corbels, cornices, and toothing stones moved slightly. Nothing returned to the way it had been before, nothing held the same place as it had, but Madame Helena, satisfied, asked the new guest to follow her and told her no, oh no, please, don't bother even with the hatbox, the maid will take it all to your rooms right away. The stones, wood, and metal became quiet; smooth water showed Katja's face leaning over it, the rag to clean the windowpanes in her hand; the house breathed, walls straightened, windows cleared, doorjambs shined, and panels gleamed. Where were they, Katja asked herself, and she answered herself with something she also could not understand: in childhood. Perhaps winged beings went there. Or perhaps not: she had heard the words, but from whom? From Luduv, of course, in her ear.

2. In Black

As always, Madame Helena wore black, although not full mourning: often with a green brooch, a golden-yellow foulard, or piping or cuffs; but of course no lace, not even as edging, enlivened the dark outfit, and she walked a step, only one step and no more to avoid seeming rude or in any way discourteous, in front of Madame Nashiru, a guide showing the way and at the same time doing justice to the house, neither too fast nor too slow, letting the new guest take in its solidity, the good taste of its decoration and lighting fixtures, and above all the exceptional quality of certain pieces of furniture, paintings, and items of porcelain or silver. In addition and with a bit of effort, she was trying not to think too much about something highly indelicate so that her face would show only friendly interest: Madame Helena wondered whether Madame Nashiru could walk as fast as she could in case she had to hurry. She had heard or read somewhere that in Japan, mothers and grandmothers, ill-natured old women drenched in their own rancor, enclosed newborn girls' feet in wooden boxes so they would not grow, and men planning to choose a wife made certain that the candidates had diminutive feet and selected the woman with the smallest ones. Did they line them up and tell them to take off their shoes? Did they say something like I love you dearly but your feet aren't small enough? Did they walk down streets and through salons with their eyes on the ground looking for the feet of their dreams? Were there contests, competitions, and prizes? Did upper-class women make use of boxes that were more discrete, lush, inlaid, carved, painted, impossible to remove, inviolable, and therefore more effective than the ones worn by poor women? Did they single out some girl at school or in parties for not having feet as small as the other girls? She had not seen Madame Nashiru's feet, hidden beneath the hem of her dress, and she would never look down to try to find out whether they were normal or frighteningly small, with her instep arched like a hump of angry flesh. Perhaps she could get a glimpse of them some night in the salon if Madame Nashiru were to cross her legs when Madame Helena was convivially passing around bonbons after dinner, or if she were to lift her dress to keep it dry as she was going out on some rainy day. Nonetheless it seemed that Madame Nashiru walked with an almost ethereal ease, and her face, when Madame Helena paused to raise a curtain or open a door, was as placid as it had been when she had crossed the entryway and offered her gloved hand. Madame Helena concluded that Madame Nashiru's feet must be normal, that no one had enclosed them in tiny wooden boxes the day she was born, she had never cried out in pain or had tried to remove the cursed binding while some old woman with tight lips advised her with secret pleasure to be patient and endure it the way she and her mother and her mother's mother had endured it; she could even accompany her to Mr. Vorge's shop, the shoemaker on Rede Street who made her shoes, and watch her display her feet without any shame when the apprentice took the measurements. Which was merely a passing thought because she would never do anything as unsuitable as be seen in the street with Madame Nashiru, that was certain, calling attention to herself in a city where so many people knew her, alongside a foreigner.

Madame Nashiru did not dress in black: she wore a two-piece mustard-yellow suit with brown piping and buttons. The collar of her jacket was open over a yellow silk blouse. Her hat, gloves, and Madame Helena supposed shoes were brown. She carried a fox muff in her right hand and a brown leather purse on her left forearm. She wore a two-strand pearl necklace and matching earrings, pearls so purely iridescent that Madame Helena had wondered, seeing them as Madame Nashiru arrived from the outdoor light, shining in the darkness of the vestibule almost with the glow of diamonds, whether they had just been taken from the sea, if they still dripped, wet and salty, onto Madame Nashiru's shoulders. Madame Nashiru smiled and nodded. She was obviously satisfied by what was to come in the house on Scheller Street.

3. Treasures

Mr. Pallud heard the women pass his
door. He heard the steps of the formidable Lundgren, mistress
owner madam and proprietress of the house, and other steps,
muffled and faint, light but not hasty or imprudent, alongside
Madame Helena's unmistakable steps; steps on a known surface,
obedient and dominated from time immemorial, steps of the type
the general might take when he went out to the field to count the
dead after a battle while he awaited the arrival of the king who
came to congratulate him for the success of the campaign—do
generals count the dead or do they assign that dirty job to their
most unlucky noncommissioned officer? In any case, the general
would not walk that other way over the field of battle or any other
ground; he would walk with a straight back, head set between raised
shoulders, eyes scornful but not moving in any direction with
respect to nearby buildings, or left or right according to who may be
speaking or coming to speak to him, but instead gazing far away at
the misty road where the king would be arriving. The conquistadors
must have strode through the New World the way Madame
Lundgren moved through her house from sidewalk to garden and
basement to mansard, Mr. Pallud was certain of that each time he
thought about the day when he would leave: with confidence and
admiration, firmly, without deceit or divine heralds or purveyors of
death, frightened but with no trace of it on his face, sporting his

worn boots and the fine tooled leather breastplate stained by sweat and wine: is it possible that I have crossed the sea, defeated scaly monsters, and traveled back here? Possible that the plants earth sky women rivers mission to propagate the true faith and the gold and the silver cities and storms belong to me? It was then that he decided that yes, he would leave, not only the house and the city but the region country continent and known world: to leave for the Americas, put his clothes and treasures in a giant trunk—and whose could be those other steps, those fickle and almost noiseless steps swallowed up by the rug, dampened by the walls, half-heard on the other side of the windowed door, whose?—to take a ship with a gold and blood-red keel and a sharp cutwater, a ship five hundred feet long, with an irascible captain, goblets of icy wine on the deck, confidantes at dawn, jackets in the afternoon, to debark in a port on the other side of the world, Lima perhaps or Buenos Aires; Buenos Aires, that's it, buildings of glass streets paved in gold brown women with swinging hips cloying music next to a warm sea. The new guest, the source of the unrecognized steps, they would be hers, the new guest who had been announced by Katja, Kati-Kati, that insolent girl who cleared away the platters and plates with an almost festive curtness, they would be hers, golden steps, no, silken uncertain steps, a lady's steps. Talkative Kati-Kati, high collar and long sleeves decreed by that Lundgren woman, but if you stretched out your hand, since in the end she was only a servant, in a move slipping down her backside toward the unobtainable, she would act as offended as if *she* were the Madame. In those distant countries of white cities populated by squat men smoking cigars beneath moustaches and enormous straw hats while they watched their women with baleful eyes, Mr. Pallud could win admiration for his bearing, his still-blond hair, his clear eyes, his fine white hands. He would open a store to display his treasures and set the prices so high no one could buy anything. He would drink sickly sweet coffee and liquors, traverse the streets beneath the sun wearing a raw silk suit leaning on a bamboo cane with a gold haft, and he would marry the heiress of some millionaire rancher who would of course be unfaithful but it would not matter to him. He would have friends. Perhaps he would hold some quasi-official position. He would acquire influence. He would be surrounded by mystery and very young girls who would serve him day and night with smiles full of bright white teeth. He hoped the new guest would be lodged one floor up in the exterior room that had been unoccupied for so long: he would prefer someone who walked lightly like young Gangulf, who moved like a fox, light like someone under suspicion, light like the sparrow hawk that hunted barely touching the ground, like a sloop that veered to catch the final wind, like the vole and the sundew, like venal sin.

Mr. Pallud's room did not face Scheller Street or the garden; it faced a side patio. Mr. Pallud spoke of "my rooms" but it was only one room with an arcade that formed something like an angle, a corner that authorized him to use the plural although it was in no way another room. There he had placed a table and around it shelves where he exhibited his treasures. He often moved them around, looked for locations more favorable to each of them when he cleaned them; he would caress them, play with them, talk to them; he would invite the other guests to look at them while he recounted where he had obtained each one, how much it had cost, how he kept it shining or soft or how he had restored it, the history he knew or imagined. The rooms, the room cut by the arcade's jambs and lintel almost in two, had very pale wallpaper, just right to reflect the light that entered through the only opening to the outside, a large window wider than it was tall in the wall opposite the door, which was also off in the corner. This window had a false balcony outside with a stone balustrade against a blind wall below the windowsill held up by small columns, nine of them, on whose curved sides were carved interlaced oak leaves. Mr. Pallud, when he took the room, had asked that the blinds and lace curtains that covered the window be removed, and although that request had seemed strange to Madame Helena, she had agreed, thinking that it was no more than the whim of a bachelor and involved no inconvenience, no risk to leave this window bare since the side patio was closed and no one could see it from a neighboring house. This false balcony and true window were well protected from sight and noise: from coach wheels on the pavement and the shouts of children who played on Scheller Street during good weather. So, without curtains, in silence, and with white walls, the room was well-lit by day and Mr. Pallud could busy himself with his treasures and fill notebooks, now about to finish the fifth one, with sketches, descriptions, and the history of each piece. At night Mr. Pallud would light a lamp on the mantel of the fireplace, pull up a chair with its back to the circle of light, and read until late. He read the seven volumes of Heindesberg about the history of toys from the neolithic to 1850 and the treatise of Des Moines about miniatures. At times he also read a copy of *The Life of Paeonius of Menda*, published in Nuremberg in 1799, by an unnamed author.

4. The House

In about 1801 a merchant dealing in fabrics named Hoenke or Hencken ordered the house built. In that same year Baron von Hardenberg, also known as Novalis, died, and as a result the businessman began to lose what little patience he had for his second son. The house was always for the wealthy, although immediately after it was finished, it seemed austere rather than modest. At the time, much was said about the fat merchant, fat in the portrait by an unknown painter who left only two letters, L and R, as a signature and an uncertain date, 1802 or 1809, on a painting that in the times of other owners wandered from basement to attic until a dealer took it, saying he knew of an American millionaire infatuated with old portraits of long-dead old men. It was said throughout the city that he placed the construction of the house in the hands of a builder who had fled the revolutionary wars to the south with his head and soul full of dreams of a Cisalpine Republic that would never come to pass, according to the local notables who assiduously participated in the salon at Ancher Inn. The builder had a twin brother who had been a glassblower and suffered from a pulmonary illness, but had neither wife nor children, and the first sketches he made for the construction of the house moved the fabric merchant to indignation: he was no fop in the French court, he said; he did not need damascene columns or pretty little stained-glass windows or curved staircases; he was only a poor merchant who needed a solid, comfortable house with large rooms, square windows, wide doorways, a large kitchen, and above all a spacious and dry basement where he could store his merchandise, and if the builder who had fled Veneto was not capable of sketching something like that, he would have to find someone else. The builder needed the fat man's money, so he promised to leave fantasies aside as ordered and consulted his brother, who lay in a bed that faced the morning sun in a home for contagious illnesses presided over by Magdalene nuns. Coughing, sunken-chested, with red rashes on his cheeks and white patches beneath his eyes, his brother told him that getting annoyed was a virtue and could say hardly anything more because he began to cough again. The builder wanted his money, the merchant wanted a suitable house, and the sick man wanted to stay alive. The Magdalene nuns prayed day and night for the reprobates, the dying, the lost, the thieves and traitors, and the sad and suffering. The sick man died gently in his sleep in the wee hours of the night when the house had just been finished. It looked somber, serious, sedate, with just a ground floor, basement, and upper floor, on the slope of Scheller Street, which was not yet called that nor was it paved: it was called Mill Alley because at its farthest end there had been a flour mill powered by a water wheel, a building that had been converted into a weaving workshop after the river's course through the city changed, drying out the pond. In spite of the mud and the distance to the market and the church, the merchant followed his tightfisted dreams, his petty interests, and the little metal voice in his ears and often in his eyes and mouth that had spoken to him upon buying the land about the advantage of being so close to where his merchandise was made. Having understood that, he envisioned the comings and goings of his servants under the wind and the sun but not the rain which could ruin the fabric, getting help for occasional hard jobs from some vagabond or beggar content with old bread and rancid cheese, with no need to pay for carts or horses since he already had enough expenses with the family coach, a white-footed horse, two dark bays, and a pinto, while bolt after bolt of fabric accumulated in the basement. The merchant rubbed his hands together: from weft and warp to his shelves, from rollers to his cashbox, from heddle to his wallet, rachet raising and lowering the battens to his utter profit. The builder went back to his homeland, and the participants at the Ancher salon shook their heads not in grief but rather with the certainty of those who knew whereof they spoke because they had been saying such things for years and had seen just how many times their predictions had come true. On the other hand, for the merchant, the mud and dreams and sleepless nights and stinginess proved him right, and he lit the house with fine oil lamps, decorated it with tapestries and carved chairs, and heated the main rooms with deep fireplaces and the bedrooms with iron braziers over a tray for ashes decorated in its center with the face of the god of fire, with flames coming out of his ears, nose, and mouth. The marriageable daughter planted a garden, telling him it would surround the house with flowers of every color, and one of these plants, useless bug-harbors according to her father, grew up to her window, which she considered a good sign; but that plant and only that one never flowered. The younger son who had wept at the death of the poet Novalis wrote pamphlets against the emperor, and the elder son insisted that Europe was exhausted, undone, finished, impoverished, and the best thing to do would be to leave for the Americas, that new world where shovels-full of gold lay on the surface of the earth, where there was joy and riches for everyone, and where one year of work would yield a lifetime of luxurious relaxation. In spite of a rich husband found for his daughter, neither the emperor nor the flowers nor the Americas interested the master of the house on Mill Alley. It was not yet Scheller Street although, since he had bought the land, it had grown to stretch beyond the workshop, curving along the river,

ANGÉLICA GORODISCHER

giving rise to spacious, sturdy, and square homes like the fabric merchant's. No one was surprised in the salon at Ancher Inn, for they knew the younger son and had predicted something like that, since he was the brunt of jokes and poetic parodies: as the result of a poorly written and designed broadsheet stuck on a wall, blundering soldiers wrecked a neighbor's door instead of knocking down the merchant's and threw everyone there in jail. The soldiers, and worse, their commanders, were not keen intellects, rather the reverse; they listened, asked to be told again what they had just heard, thought about it, asked for clarifications, insisted that they had not been mistaken, and listened yet again and tried to understand; meanwhile the merchant had time to turn almost all his possessions into gold, haul his sons to the border disguised as coachmen, but first he delivered his marriageable daughter to the manager of the workshop with a nuptial contract stipulating that the house would always be hers and he could not sell it without her consent; and after that, no one was sure where he went. Later it was said he had gone to Cajamarca or Catamarca, one of those cities in South America in the middle of the Amazon where gold, diamonds, fevers, exotic fruits, grains and fibers, and slaves and fragrant wood appeared out of thin air. The girl was fourteen years old and the workshop manager sixty-three. She was as tightfisted as her father, but from her mother, who had died giving birth, she had been brought into the world with a bit of a taste for beauty intensified by her brother's madly written odes imitating Novalis which he had read to her at night in secret, very late, by candlelight. She had not wanted to listen to them, she only wanted to slumber, warm under the covers, her head on the pillow, asleep, but the words crept in as she drowsed and perhaps her eyes saw them, ears heard them, fingertips touched them, and dreams held them captive, so she did not forget them—not only that, they burst forth the next day in plans and projects. Probably she was not happy but the workshop owner got richer and

14

richer and had earlier been married to a woman who had died without producing children: now he had a young wife with a full belly and breasts and an imagination blind and deaf to impossibility. He planted trees in front of the south facade that faced the alley, added an extra floor for servants, and installed a garden for her and the children, seven of them, of whom four survived. The workshop owner did not meet his seventh child, one of the long-lived ones. He awoke one night with horrible pains in his chest and arms and was ill for four days, during which they bled him, gave him warm dressings and mustard plasters and salves, murmured incantations, prayed the Rosary, chilled his feet and warmed his abdomen, gave him strong drink and bauhinia extract, all useless because on the fourth day, to his sorrow, fighting to keep his soul, he gave it up to the Lord. The widow was still young, pink and plump, with a generous mouth, eyes like her visionary brother, and blond hair down to her belt which she tied in a wide bun at the back of her neck held by hairpins of fine metal and stones. She bore her seventh child amid unwanted pity, nursed him and called him all the names that she had stopped calling the other children as they grew, careful not to use the names she had invented for the children no longer there, while she administered the workshops and counted the money that kept accumulating. Ancher Inn got new owners, and those who used to meet in its salon every night dispersed toward the neighborhoods surrounding the market: there was no one to shake his head predicting misfortune. The widow married again, to a young man this time, rich but not as rich as she was, who took her to live in Kiel. They loaded up everything they had, which was a lot—children, furniture, servants, clothing, animals—and they left. The house remained, which she did not wish to sell.

The house stood empty for ten years until the city authorities decided to demolish it, but not without first publishing official notices calling for its owners or heirs. No one answered: perhaps no one found out; perhaps the heirs did not know, being as they were far away, that the house their grandfather had built so many years earlier when the *Rheinischer Merkur* was published, Novalis died, and the Peace of Lunéville was signed, was in danger. It remained standing nonetheless; in spite of conspiracies, desperation, the long dark night of the empire and the color of the horizon, it remained solidly, squarely standing, windows covered, blind and mute, with weeds snaking around it, stained by rain but upright, until the municipality thought better and decided to install its land and civil registry offices there. Mill Alley became Scheller Street, after someone whose memory had been revived, and paving stones covered the mud, for the world had begun to transform itself. They cleaned the house but did no more; no decorations, no plants that climbed to the balconies, no tapestries or curtains or fine furniture; just a waiting room, a place to spend time, to sit without speaking in drowsiness if not sleep without dreams, the useless activity of useless little men who looked at nothing and if they had looked would have seen nothing, hoping to capture, trap, and fool death.

So when the municipality sold some of its properties, it was a naked, hard body, a stranger in the landscape that was changing, attentively echoing what had once and always happened, voices and footsteps, misfortunes, foolishness, cries of newborns, ambitions stained by the sublime, and even the heavy shadow of Novalis. It was bought by a magistrate known throughout the region for his wisdom and turn of phrase, his activities in the Progressive Party, and the beauty of his wife. Strangely, and against the grain of its history, the house took on French airs: overelaborate iron balconies, a mansard, terraces, gay gardens, and gaslights appeared; curtains and rugs, fringed embroidered tapestries, crystal, molding, and gilt vases to flank the doors. The bureaucratic furniture disappeared and what replaced it had slim arched feet and springy seats covered by silky fabric. The mirrors and paintings multiplied, and once a week music played and songs were sung in the salon, and twice a year guests arrived in sparkling coaches pulled by bright-maned horses with colored ribbons braided into their tails, horseshoes sparking on the stones of Scheller Street; women dressed in gauze and velvet danced with men in elaborate uniforms gleaming with medals, epaulettes, and braiding. No one was further from the fat Hoenke than this polished and smiling master of the house who quoted Blum and Ruge and supported Stephen Born and danced with the wife of a member of the Assembly without losing sight of the groups that continued to cluster in the salon and thought about the advantages he could take from the smiles and the conversations coming to life there. No one could have been more different from the cloth merchant than this rash polemicist, good Catholic, and member of the Grossdeutsche, who talked about federalism, the Volkgeist, and the Malmoe armistice with the men; about Pergolesi, George Sand, and Werther with the women. And yet, despite the differences, across the years and shadows, they would have understood each other, sympathized, and exchanged winks and gestures of recognition: they would have felt themselves accomplices in their appetites, determination, and certainty that they were going to achieve their plans. The fat merchant had been defeated by a crazed and melancholy son; the magistrate would be defeated by a financial crisis and marital misfortune. One of the daughters of the beautiful wife and the magistrate married a banker and remained in the house when her mother went to live in London and her brothers married and bought other houses. It did not matter to her that one winter day dawned with her father hanging from a beam in the mansard, his face violet, his feet bare, swinging, his neck held by his own belt, pushed by the wind blowing through the open windows; or perhaps she believed it was her duty to remain, or she felt closer to her childhood there, safekeeping the death of her father, or she wished to remember it every morning by holding it so near, or to forget it by keeping it too near to be seen. The daughter was named Hebe, a Greek name that meant precisely *young daughter*, the little girl of the house; and her husband, bearded and very rich, was named Heinrich-Marie-Joszef. She would have scorned the fat, greedy merchant who had built the house where she lived: she would not have honored him with a greeting if she had passed him in the avenue in the new park, he in a coach with a running board, she in a light calash, he dressed in dark clothing, cape, and wide-brimmed hat, she in white with sea-green ribbons, hat held with gold pins, and lace parasol. She would not even have looked at him, could not have been his accomplice in the shadows as her father could have been. But she knew nothing of all this. She knew her husband was one of the richest men in the city and because of that, she, her sons, her daughters, and her house had to be the handsomest in the city. She knew she liked to get up late, bathe and wear perfume, call on friends, play whist, go out with her sons and especially her daughters who looked so much like her, host dinners and parties, go to the theater, sit beneath the trees in the garden in summer and next to the fire in the hearth in winter, travel, listen to popular singers, and be accustomed to expensive dresses. Once she felt doubts, or a cloud, hiatus, or ice made her pause, overcome by a step into emptiness; once a question harried her or time betrayed her; the shadow of the young goddess laughed instead of her, the little girl of the house; the world swayed as her father had swayed in the wind hung on his own belt, and life lost its shape and became useless, without width, substance, destiny, something she could release without anyone realizing she no longer held it, and she asked: Am I dying now, is there nothing more, and if not, what mark, what trace, what clue, what vestige, what hint will remain, what can I do, who would remember me for just one day; and in this final moment what am I myself going to remember: travel, men, dances, dresses, parties, monsters, jungles, my father, earthquakes, or playing cards, wine, tears, beings with leathery wings who dance in a too-cold wind, bottomless abysms to fall into? And she said no, oh no, please no, but it was no more than a second, less then a second before taking another step down the staircase, getting into the coach, and leaving. That night she docilely let her husband take her and he thought that she seemed too complacent, so much that perhaps she had a lover and felt guilty; but he looked at her and as he did, he remembered so many of the things that he had said about her that it could not be, for she did not have the stuff for a sustained lie, she was stupid, very beautiful and very stupid, to his good luck. And the next morning as he left he spent a moment looking at the house and the street on which it stood and thought about his wife, about how submissive and delicate she had been, and, smiling, he gave an order to the groom. He rode proudly down Scheller Street next to the river with its white mansions and groves of trees and gardens traversed by coaches like his pulled by English or Arabic horses, and lit by gas streetlights at night. He thought he could spend his whole life there and die there, but that was not the case. They sold the house eighteen years later when their youngest daughter, the one who looked most like her mother, married, and they went to live in Berlin where Heinrich-Marie had interests in several new stock investment funds. They left the house sadly: for a moment before the move certain memories regathered strength but faded in the haste of preparations, broke into ever more pale pieces trapped in corners, on the roof, in the opening of a door, and the shadow of the transom, and died abandoned when the last coach left. The name of the new owner was Lundgren, of Swedish extraction, great-grandson of the poet Asa Lundgren and a distant relative, according to him, of the founder of Lund. His father had arrived in the city on a business trip and had never returned to Sweden: there he had stayed, there he had married, there he had worked and had amassed a discrete fortune; there he had had five children, had seen them grow and learn, marry and have children; and there he had died a few years previous, six months after his wife. The Lundgrens had a daughter whose name was also Greek but in no way resembled the banker's wife, that little girl of the house always young, guardian of her father's death, perhaps because launching a thousand ships is very different from remaining the same today as yesterday and the day before yesterday and the same tomorrow as today and yesterday. When the first telephones were installed and the electric locomotive began to propel itself and Maddox tested silver nitrate plates, when *Das Kapital* and *On the Origin of Species by Means of Natural Selection* were published, when an anxious young man in Vienna composed his *Letter about Graduation to Emile Baron Fluss*, when the torpedo and reinforced concrete were invented, the parents of Helena Lundgren celebrated the wedding of their daughter with a party in the house on Scheller Street. The husband was an Austrian doctor, fifteen years older than she was, who took her to live in Linz. He had seen a serious and strong girl, decisive and discrete, dressed in light blue; a quiet and unexcitable girl who did not dance well or laugh hard but walked directly without waving her arms or hands, and he had thought she would be the best person to wait for him at home after he did his rounds or his shift in a hospital ward; she would be there, without questions or expecting too much from him; she would smile little and ask for little. She had seen him as a stranger, someone distant, as hidden as treasures buried by the corsairs on the beaches of Tortuga; a solid and unexpected man whom she would discover little by little until she reached the most precious gold at the bottom of a chest battered by time; someone who, reluctant at first but later agreeable, would let her share his dreams and desires; someone who would provide water for her fantasies so she could bathe in them and emerge as a different person, dressed in the most exquisite gold. Helena Lundgren thought she had lived just for that, for that moment when, at a gathering of young people, she had seen him talking with a friend's father on the other side of the salon while she was dancing with someone more than forgettable. The married couple received magnificent gifts because Mr. Lundgren was well-connected to wealthy local families, and they left that same night by train. Mrs. Lundgren wept a little, but Mr. Lundgren told her, come now, come now; the guests went home and the servants washed the tablecloths and shook out the rugs.

The Danube could be seen from the windows of the second floor of the doctor's house, but a cigar factory impregnated the air, irritating eyes and noses, especially on windy days. Her husband had an office on the first floor and Helena was bored upstairs with the windows closed. She did not like to sew, embroider, or paint with watercolors; she had a servant, a cook, and a young girl who came to help with the cleaning; the house was tidy and orderly, the closets smelling of lavender, the bathroom of mint, and the drawing room of wood; the platters shone and the crystal rang. She had large, strong hands, amazon legs, and nervous eyes: she opened the curtains and looked out at the street, but that was not enough. Her husband did not let her go out or receive visitors or find some task, some distraction, which she had initially found flattering because she had thought he wanted her exclusively, everything for him. But he was sullen, and she could not overcome the distance between them; he wanted her to always be there, always, but not to be a bother, not to speak to him or want him to speak to her; at times he did not even look at her for hours, an afternoon, all day. He became impossible when she asked for money, every little trifle irritated him, and he would spend days without speaking to her, coming and going as if he lived alone in that house. One morning during breakfast she finally looked at him carefully, as if she had never seen him before, not even having seen him for the first time across the salon where young people had met that afternoon; she looked at him while he drank his coffee, not looking up, she looked at him slowly, in detail, his hair, his forehead, his temples, his nose and so on down his face, his neck, his arms, his entire rigid body sitting at a table like a doll with hinges. She looked at his hands, she moved in her seat to look at his waist, his hips, his thighs, she knelt to look at his feet, and then she straightened up and thought about the razor-edged instruments in the cabinet in his office: with one of those sharp blades she could make in incision from his forehead and down down down the same way she had looked at him, she could study him from inside, too, separate gray or pinkish warm viscera from the yellow fat that surrounded them, wet her fingers with blood and thick fluids until she found the gold. In her jaw and then in her entire mouth she felt the sweet aftertaste of expectation, the hope of something long desired. The woman who had launched a thousand ships had done absolutely nothing except leave her house, and because of that she did not move from her chair, and she let him go without saying a word. When she was alone in the dining room, she thought about the house that her parents had bought, a house from which she could not see the Danube but instead a tree-lined street, a different river, a garden, and other houses; she thought about the room with the balcony that faced the crowns of the trees, she thought about a tree filled with white flowers, and that was the moment when she got up, opened the windows of the dining room and let the irritating air inside. She went to the bedroom, opening the windows as she passed them, packed her suitcase, put on a light blue suit, went down the stairs, and left, also without saying a word.

Until then all the women who had lived in the house on Scheller Street could have been a single woman who had wound up leaving it for another country, another city, another house, after having eaten, slept, and borne children in it. They had left alone or with their husbands, and they had left nothing behind of themselves.

Helena Lundgren was the one who returned: she had briefly had a man at her side, she had not borne children, she had left and had decided to return, and when she inherited the house she had decided, against all advice, against sensibility and self-interest, that she did not want to sell it and look for smaller one or an apartment in the center of the city, that she wanted to do something with it, not knowing what. She walked from one end to the other, she touched it, she went around corners, she pondered it, she slept on it, and she sat in the grand salon on the ground floor and reflected on it. The tea, the dark oblique mirror in the cup, steaming on a cold afternoon, showed her the reflection of lamplight as if it were a drop of yellow paint. She told herself that now she knew what she had known without knowing it. She put the cup on the table and walked through the house again with a notebook, writing down the modifications that she would have to make.

5. Lola Is Cooking

Before the clock in the salon rings eight in the morning, every morning the steps of Madame Helena strike the marble in the service stairway, continue down, become loud on the wood floor, pause on the checkerboard mosaic but never pass beyond the green and black border that marks the edge of the pantry, and Lola waits for her on the other side of the border, closer to the kitchen door but not much closer, in a sky blue dress and blue apron, arms crossed and hands in her pockets. Stew pot, frying pan, copper-bottomed pots, saucepan, stock pot, saute pan, blue eyes, untidy black hair tied with a yellow-and-pink-striped scarf, the oven lit, the burners revived by clumsy-handed Wulda waving a reed fan. Madame Helena is the first to say good morning and Lola answers; then Lola is the first to speak and Madame Helena chooses what will be served that day at noon and evening while Lola imagines knife, cleaver, meat tenderizer, and colander on the table; while Lola sniffs, looks, separates, and distributes eggs and mushrooms, thyme and sage, scallions and cheese, mint and rosemary, milk, ginger, oregano, galanga, ground pepper always white, leavening and citron, garlic, beans and vinegar, parsley, paprika, curry and a pinch of sugar mixed with sesame. Madame Helena leaves, making much less noise than descending, and succulent Lola turns toward the kitchen and moves forward with sails set but very little cable freed from the anchor's windlass, shaking her head with resignation at Wulda's efforts: Lola keeper of the embers, Lola, whose veins are swollen with broth, liquor, juice, strong hot coffee, and sweet wines, says oh girl, oh, and tells Wulda that from the looks of things, if she does not pay attention, she will never learn anything.

Lola comes from the east, from the plains of hunger and persecution; she came from death, slowly, not running but now laughing and she is a cook because what other thing can be done in this world where if you look around you will see that everyone eats, men, women, animals, time, everything. She learned to cook from a grandmother who was killed when she ran off toward the forest and for that she got not even a burial: Lola thought she knew everything and escaped with nothing. She crossed the border by pure luck behind the backs of armed men and begged in the city at the doors of a café which she entered one night because, as she told a man dressed in solid black who happened to ask her why, outside it was cold but inside it was warm. The cook laughed and asked her if she knew how to poach eggs. She said yes and that night she slept indoors and the next day she ate three meals and when, five years later, she left the job of head cook to work in the boarding house on Scheller Street with less bustle and better pay, she had plumped up to one hundred seventy pounds, married, had a son who died at birth and because of that had no more menstrual periods, separated from her husband, and knew everything she had thought she had known at the edge of the forest.

The biggest room under the mansard is Lola's: big enough for a double bed, night table, large chest, closet, table, and two chairs. She has a mirror and a rug, a heating stove and a curtain on the oval window. On the wall at the head of the bed hangs a colored print of Saint Elizabeth of Schuange in ecstasy. There is a coat hook behind the door and a landscape of Bavaria in an old gold frame on the wall opposite the bed. Lola keeps blankets, sheets, and heavy winter coats in the chest; her dresses in the left side of the closet, the aprons, caps, and underwear on the right, and a gold chain with a gold heart that has a shining stone in the center wrapped in a handkerchief inside a shoe she no longer uses mixed in with other shoes on the floor of the closet. Sometimes on Sunday nights after having left everything prepared to start the week's work the next day, she locks the door of her room, descends the service stairways silently, and leaves. She sits drinking a beer in a tavern near the river where the owner has known her for years, ever since she was a kitchen porter, assistant cook, and finally head cook at Café Netzel, and she carefully looks one by one at the regular customers without haste, as if she were sizing them up, trying to get it right, as if she were playing—that one? No, not that one, his eyes are too close together and his shirt cuffs are dirty, this other one? Hmmm, could be, I like him, big hands, or maybe not, let's see, that one? Yes, that one, or no, better the other one with the big hands and long legs to wrap around her and plenty of laughter to recall on nights that are not Sunday, he is happy, I will, no, I won't, I hope he turns around; another beer. In the rooms upstairs, she likes to release all that flesh, to open her blouse and laugh, imagine that it is not just that one who opens his mouth wide for sweets, he who surrounds her with his tongue and hands, but all of them, all the men in the world, those she had and those she did not and even the one that she left downstairs with his eyes too close together and his dirty shirt cuffs, all of them, those who can and those who no longer can, old men, thin men, young men, very young, athletes, teachers, sailors, fat men, blonds, merchants, sad men, dying men, rich men, madmen, poor men, powerful men, all, all of them, they all take her and lick her and lay her down over the bed and submerge and rise up only to breathe and return to her, all of them, not just that one and she is happy, broth and onion, wine and butter, ginger, bread, liquor. Lola does not know about Madame Nashiru; she continues to talk to Wulda as she passes white shelves, opens and closes doors, slides boxes, says that it is the hand that should move, not the arm, takes out the whisk, knives, cutting board, large tongs, peeler, spatula, sieve and cooking pot, two enameled casseroles, a pitcher, teaspoon and tablespoon. She tells Wulda that if her arm moves she will get tired, it is better to relax the elbow and shoulder, move your head like this as if you were singing and it would not be bad to sing, relax the neck and only your hand is left, as if it is someone else's and not yours, moving the fan hey-ho hey-ho so that the fire dances. She says all this while she places the meat, fish, greens, nuts, cream, salt, butter, and spices on the table, and she tells her to write in the notebook that they need to buy beets, powdered French mustard, rice, and oil, and that they have to order white cheesecloth because what they have is hardly any good anymore, and a curved wide-eyed round-tip needle.

What Lola does know is that there is a new guest who is going to stay six months at least and knows nothing more until Wulda, tired and stiff without understanding much about only the hand, tells her the guest is a strange woman, she saw her when she got out of the coach and she is so strange she will want to eat strange things. On the basement windowsill sit flowerpots with plants Lola brings home sometimes when she has to go out: she waters them with a white crockery pitcher that says in black letters *Two Liters. Not For Commercial Use.* Lola, fat and humming, thinks that Madame Helena said nothing about the strange guest to her, or no, what matters for Wulda is to be able to rest this arm that moves around too much and uses too much energy, and while Madame Helena may not have said anything to her, all strange women will be strange upstairs, but down here like everyone else, hake with nut sauce and vegetables, veal steaks cooked in gravy, a cup of light broth, and seasonal fruit with iced whipped cream, each item on its proper platter so Katja dressed in black, white apron white cap and gloves, will take it to the table right on the hour. Lola tells Wulda that there among the plants is a creeper and Wulda asks what is a creeper and Lola tells her but what a silly girl, a creeper is something that creeps, that only knows how to creep, that lives to creep, on a balcony, on a flagstaff, on a column, on the trunk of a tree, and even on a wire if you know how to hang it right. She also tells her she knows she is tired but she is not going to relieve her of that task and maybe she will learn to leave her hand loose, just her hand as if it were not hers and like this to fan the fire without getting tired. But it does not take long for her to feel sorry for her, poor thing, poor little thing, and tells her it is all right, stop now, the fire will not die, and give herself a massage on the arm with the other hand. In this country the creepers wrap this side around but in other countries on the other side of the world they wrap around the other side around, and this is a mystery. Wulda looks and looks at her, cannot stop looking at her, rubbing her left hand up and down her right arm again and again—how can that be? Lola tells her that absolutely anything is possible, that the world is great big crouching animal and who knows if the bottom half of the big animal is doing the opposite of the upper part of the big animal. Wulda stops rubbing her left hand on her right arm and before Lola starts talking again asks her if the world might be two big crouching animals one against the other each one wrapped in creepers from whatever side they want without knowing what the other animal is doing. Lola fans the fire, which dances, and Lola, laughing, says yes, it could be, but she is going to plant this creeper in the garden, and covers the fire with an iron grille and flames try to rise above it and now cannot. Wulda puts away the reed fan and asks if the two big animals have their eyes shut. Lola says she does not know but their mouths are open and they eat. She knows how the world eats, how it chews and swallows and drinks, how it stuffs itself at food stands and how it chows down in dives and how it savors in salons and opens its barrier of teeth and raises silverware full of food to its mouth and how it wipes its mouth with a napkin and how the people upstairs sigh before they get up from the table; the man with the toys eats exactly like the mechanical bird that Katja told her he has on his shelf and pecks on the wood eighteen times, Katja counted, each time he pulls the cord, but eats nothing; the boy, young man, whatever, eats without paying attention to the texture or temperature or taste when he eats and at times does not eat and stares into space as if his mind and stomach were elsewhere; Miss Esther calm and so quiet that if you were to see her you would let her take communion without confession sipping her wine between courses; the fat woman complaining and her daughter jumpy when they come down to the dining room but Wulda says that if she takes trays to their room it is the same; the soldier so fast that you cannot see how the knife and fork and spoon move; Madame Helena like a lady savoring every bite speaking little and listening to everything. The fat hisses in the saucepan over the fire, the oily yellow nuts are crushed in Wulda's hands, but she does not know that a bread tree grows in the navel of the world.

6. Tea

At teatime, however, silence served as protection; an artificial stillness imposed itself on the house as if an external, isolating unction had occupied and transformed it into something more like a temple or exile than dwelling place. In any case, something had changed: if at any previous moment water had boiled or a pot had struck a stove burner, if knives had rattled in the drawer before being placed on the tablecloth, at the moment when the tea was drunk, everything became hushed, Wulda dozed, Lola did the accounts, and Katja stepped carefully. In no other moment reigned so much silence: not at night, as one by one the remaining lights went out, eyes closed, and breathing slowed under blankets, nor at morning with bodies yet to awake and move. While the guests and servants respected the silence, no one appreciated it like Madame Helena; voices and noise were subdued, and no one knew like her the house from end to end to reckon those changes without seeing them, the surprise of hours, the laziness of minutes, the exact place where the shadow of a doorjamb reached on that month day and instant of the year even if there were no sunshine to reveal where it would have been, the size of a crack in the herringbone parquet in a hallway, as if objects that could be displaced or removed or acquired mattered much less. Most of the day, however, was not that way; the time before lunch seemed to run counter to the peace of the afternoon, or even the most perfect

Sunday because Sundays lay smooth and empty, a waiting blue hollow in which, although no one said so, a long series of events availed itself to the truce of an imperfect memory. The worst part of the day, like a pendulum or opposing force, a reliable balance to the still and hushed mid-afternoon maintained and imposed by the house, was the time before the evening meal when the day was over and done and could not be brought back except long afterward when defections and failures were no longer so indelible: a time when something halfway done could not be finished, much less could something be started anew, an impatient time when remorse or annoyance stretched out, fingers fidgeted in pockets, hands took things from their places and put them back like inopportune memories or the indecision that undid deeds: come on, finish it or give it up or let it be tomorrow already.

In the afternoons during good weather when the shouts of neighbors' children playing in Scheller Street could be heard in almost the farthest corner of the house, in the afternoons Katja would bring up a china platter covered by a white napkin and nothing else because Madame Helena's imperious furnishings held an entire tea service and teapot with its heater already over the marble-topped table. Katja knocked on the door and waited for Madame Helena to open it or give her permission to open the door and enter, and every day during this bothersome interval she tried to adopt a friendly and willing but not servile attitude thanks to which Madame would tell just by looking at her that she was good and proper, someone without strange thoughts intervening in what others would never say was there; nothing perturbed her, and not only that, she felt a certain satisfaction in herself since she knew how to fulfill her duties well, while she watched her hands on the sides of the platter so that only the thumbs were visible, the fingers on the china hidden under the napkin, trying to remember if she had stuffed all her hair, all of it, under the cap, thinking about

Wulda almost without trying, the way someone can blow out a candle without thinking, or put a key in a lock without thinking, or clean one's shoes on a doormat without thinking, because earlier, by earlier meaning her first days in the boarding house on Scheller Street, Wulda was the one who brought the platter with the hot little sesame-seed breadsticks or the soft rolls with butter or whatever Lola had prepared for the afternoon; but one day two or three weeks after she had started, when she was still unsure of herself and trying to learn whether she would be staying or going, Madame Helena had come down to the kitchen at a time when she never appeared there, at two or three in the afternoon, and Lola, sitting at a white table covered with a white tablecloth writing down what she needed to buy in a notebook, had looked at her strangely and had not stood up: she had only stopped moving her hand on the white paper and waited. Madame Helena had said from that day on she, Katja, would be the one to carry the china platter up to her room in the afternoon, and only then had Lola stood up and said yes, from this afternoon, Madame, Katja will bring up the platter and not Wulda, and everyone had been very happy with that change, especially Wulda.

The afternoon of the day Madame Nashiru arrived at the boarding house on Scheller Street had been as quiet as it had become every afternoon since Madame Helena had taken over the house and turned it into the most elegant boarding house in the city. She imagined Madame Nashiru already unpacking in her rooms, suitcases open, things strewn about, where else but on the bed, the dressing table and the chest of drawers: dresses, coats, underclothing on chairs, open drawers, letters, gloves, photographs, but her jewelry already put away, and her shoes? perhaps barefoot on the bedroom rug with feet that she had not seen and did not want to think about—and Madame Helena stood to one side so Katja could enter through the door that she had just opened. Katja left the platter on the table and asked as always if Madame needed anything more and Madame Helena said no and thanked her and Katja left.

Some guests were in the dining room drinking tea or hot chocolate or coffee according to their preferences; young Gangulf had not arrived nor had Madame Esther, and Katja had to go down to the kitchen and come back up to bring tea to fat Simeoni and her daughter. Two cups with their saucers, a platter with little browned loaves, butter, marmalade, cheese, two French rolls, two glasses, a pitcher of water, teapot, sugar bowl, milk, cream, knives, spoons, tongs for the sugar, a wand to stir the tea, napkins, strainer, and lemon candies: she did not know how she could manage to carry up so much without exhaustion, climb the stairs without dropping anything, milk, china, water, and honey spilling on the stairway, the rug stained, the tray rolling down and destroying the afternoon silence like maddened drums. She told Lola she did not know how to carry up all that, and Lola laughed and told her exercise would be good for her, it would make her arms fleshy and robust and men liked that, the plump arms of a girl who worked, not those weak things of a consumptive little lady, but all that meant nothing because Lola always laughed and encouraged her and Wulda.

Almost as if Madame Helena were not there, as if she had gone out, as if she were not on the other side of her door sitting and drinking tea: it occurred to no one to call on her, visit her, or even think about her; downstairs some guests read, others spread marmalade on hot bread without looking; upstairs Madame Sophie scolded her daughter, who did not want to look down the hall to see if Katja was arriving with the tray, and the daughter stubbornly replied that it was still early. Madame Helena, sitting at the table with the marble top, waited for the tea to steep in the teapot. She had become fond of tea after she married; when she was young she never drank tea, then it had tasted as bitter as illness, the scent as thick as fever, the taste like pain and the lethargic weight of convalescence; it smelled of weakness, closed windows, low lights, and whispering. But in Linz the smell of coffee was mixed with the odor of the tobacco plant that riled her stomach and kept her trapped more than a malady would, so behind the windowpanes and the lace curtains she began to drink tea and kept drinking it after all that had ceased to be important to her: in the afternoon she prepared a full pot of tea and knew that when it was ready Katja would knock on the door carrying a platter with freshly baked rolls or bread, not because Katja was punctual but Lola was, as she had said when she had come to discuss employment. If a cook does not smell good, is not punctual, fast, tidy, happy, and a little impertinent, Lola had told her, she would not do as a cook; she might know how to cook but would not do as a cook, and sooner or later that would be obvious; Madame Helena had liked those opinions and had preferred Lola to the first assistant from the kitchen of the former Bieder house, who came magnificently recommended, because he was thin, bilious, and bald and had a sad face; just because of that and his way of dressing, and she had not been wrong. She poured the tea and it fell like a coppery stream into the white cup, and the steam rose up in a sudden, aromatic caress thick with herbs and smoke. She drank tea very hot without sugar, not like the Simeonis who used milk, honey, cream, sugar, boiling water, lemon, and whatever else occurred to them at the time until it became something that was not tea and, she supposed, they complained and fought while they drank the now lukewarm liquid. Tea and silence: in Japan, and it seemed to her that she had heard or read that in other Oriental countries as well, teatime was surrounded by a grand ceremony, a ritual that had to do with religion or love or both. If she were to ask Madame Nashiru about this, it would not be indiscreet, in fact, this question could lead to an interesting conversation for everyone that would have nothing to do with feet locked into boxes or those women who play lutes and recite poems in houses of ill repute. She had not been able to get pearl tea but what she ought not to do was ask Madame Nashiru about the pearls she used, although she had told her she drank any kind of tea, green or black, and Madame Helena had wondered how that could be. Would Madame Nashiru be down there having tea with the General and Mr. Pallud? Would young Gangulf arrive in time for a cup of tea today? The tea ceremony would include, how could it not, silence; not silence like the silence in the house in the afternoon but a silence with the rustle of silk or the beating of wings. She brushed away a dream with the wave of a hand, a sip, a movement of her head: the dream in which a woman walked barefoot in the shadows of a bamboo and paper room, trembling because she did not wish to but she would submit, while in the darkness someone waited for her, rapacious, brushing his trophy with the tips of his claws.

7. Awakening

Barely dawn, Lola in the kitchen brushing aside ashes, reviving the fire, Katja opening the lower floor windows, Wulda more quiet than at any other time knocking on the service door, sleeping standing up if she could, if she knew that Katja had not heard her and was coming to open it; a little later but not much, the noise of china, knives, decanting liquids; Miss Esther being the first to enter the dining room, sometimes finishing breakfast and leaving before anyone else had arrived; before the clock in the salon struck eight, Madame Helena coming down to the kitchen; and perhaps at or about this moment Mr. Pallud entering the dining room nose to the wind detecting breezes and the smell of coffee; the General returning from his hike; and then the Simeonis coming down when they came down to breakfast since they did not always come down, indeed, as Madame Sophie's health deteriorated, more and more frequently they remained upstairs, calling and waiting for trays to be brought up to their rooms; just before nine Madame Helena appearing in the dining room, and then, eager and smiling, the last one to arrive, strange because a student ought to be in class or at his books at dawn, young Gangulf seeking his strong black bitter coffee and, as if guilty, drinking it quickly without eating anything, saying good-bye and leaving even before Madame Helena sat, and breakfast service waited until she had finished and left to patrol the house looking at everything, checking, watching, listening, and touching, at times calling to point out was needed at that moment in the morning as people left the house: Madame Helena doing her duties as lady of the house, visiting the plumber or lawyer or wallpaper shop, going to the bank or upholsterer, Lola in the market buying parsnips or a half-peck of durum wheat flour or ordering claret wine since it was about to run out, the General marching toward the Army Museum, young Gangulf to the university, Miss Esther to "Miraflora," but Mr. Pallud in slippers shut inside his room diligently cleaning and arranging his treasures, Nehala and her mother arguing over a pillow Madame Sophie wanted a little lower, not that much, on the side, there, there where her back hurt so much and her daughter ought to know where it hurt unless she was doing that intentionally, Katja and Wulda cleaning, scrubbing, shaking, polishing, progressing up and down without pause until the time when everyone except often young Gangulf and Miss Esther started arriving for lunch, when Katja changing in her bedroom watched herself reflected in the glass of the open windows against the dark wall, and Wulda, settling into the kitchen, adjusted her apron and looked at Lola, looked at her, as if by looking at her she would hear her better, and felt hunger creeping in through her nose, sauces as porous as tulle arriving through her eyes, golden broths making her mouth water, meat the color of pressed grapes in summer dropping into her stomach, silver and marble fish dancing in her belly, rosy and jasmine creams, come on girl pay attention or you'll burn your fingers and the devil will get the chance to put his hand under your petticoats; and upstairs conversations measuring words against the clatter of cutlery, Madame Helena presiding over a long table with a white tablecloth and chalk-colored dishes with a border of Amadou-style twining rosy birdweed branches that she treasured although it was no longer in style.

After lunch once again the house emptying itself of noise, voices, and movement, purring only in the kitchen and in the Simeonis's rooms, the General absorbed in some battle plan, Mr. Pallud dozing in his armchair, Madame Helena balancing the books; culminating in rest, in the silence of teatime and beyond that, the house and with it its inhabitants waking only close to dinnertime, Katja lighting the lamps in the salon, each one coming downstairs feeling uneasy, appearing in vain at the double doors because they had to wait patiently for the arrival of Madame Helena once again presiding over a snowy-white table at night with a silver centerpiece, suggesting a discussion topic, asking a question, the General clearing his throat, always falling into the trap, the Simeonis very close together on the other side of the table, asking each other questions, back and forth, answering each other, complaining quietly, Katja entering with trays and bottles and clean plates but then, unlike after breakfast, the house did not quiet down but instead lit up, bright and lively in the salon, the guests conversing, Madame Helena offering bonbons, Katja bringing liquors in etched bottles with silver necks, someone laughing, proposing a game, and finally arising and wishing good night, little by little and one by one others doing the same and from there on the house becoming hushed, lights being put out, doors closed, windows shuttered, and only a creak, a rustle, a murmur, and the dominion of dreams.

8. The Forest of Birch Trees

Every morning, hungry for battle, the General embarked on a long march from Scheller Street to Krieger Park that took him ninety minutes and for which he arose at six fifteen when it was still night in winter and day had broken in summer. The General's room did not have a window with the luxurious false exterior balcony like the one Mr. Pallud occupied in the middle of the hall: his had only one paltry window that opened into an airshaft facing the blind wall of the house next door and allowed a little sunshine to enter, a bit more in summer when it was less needed and close to midday when it was more of a bother than a convenience. Neither sun nor light mattered to the General: he had not had the curtains removed and although he slept summer and winter with the glass panes open and closed them when he left to keep out bugs and dirt, he never looked out and did not need light at all. He dressed in the dark because he knew perfectly well where he had left each item of clothing before he went to bed: pants, socks, shirt, vest, tie, jacket, every accessory, belt, gloves, hat, shoes, every detail, glasses, keys, shoehorn, and wallet. He placed his folded pajamas on the bed and left in darkness for the hallway. The glass doors that faced the garden let in a little light, a gray luster that struck the rug and with great effort rose up on the walls but never reached very high. In the light shining off the plaster, the General entered the bathroom, relieved himself, washed his face and hands, brushed his teeth, moistened his hair and combed it, and left without returning to his bedroom; he left with a pace barely slower and more careful than the one which in six minutes he would use on Scheller Street toward Muse Avenue. He considered the way he moved, dressed, avoided making noise, and maintained everything orderly as important steps in everyday life that should be performed without distraction; punctuality was a cardinal virtue along with prudence, justice, strength, and temperance, but also the highest virtue if that were possible because while the others were mere outward appearances, punctuality could not be concealed and never feigned: at six thirty-four he unlocked the chancel door, at six thirty-five he opened the door to the street, he closed it, and he left. He arrived at Krieger Park at seven twelve, walked down the cinder-covered paths, entered the grove of birch trees, went around the fountain, climbed up to the pergola, came down again, and traversed the walkways, and at seven twenty-eight he returned, arriving at Scheller Street at eight and entering the dining room to have breakfast at five after eight.

The arrival of a new guest did not bother him nor was he bothered that Madame Helena had provided her with the large suite that faced the garden, the best of the house, with her own bath, four windows and a glass door to the gallery and the terrace, according to the servant girl. He had nothing to do with those people, and even less with a foreign woman who fortunately was not French, something which would have made him obliged to force Madame Helena to choose between himself and the interloper and to leave the house if its lady were disposed toward that woman, but, almost worse although it required no action on his part, she was a female of a race destined to serve and obey. The General greeted Mr. Pallud because he could not fail to do so: Pallud was a habitually disorganized man so sometimes they coincided and met in a doorway or one of them arrived at the bathroom while the other was leaving. He respected Madame Helena as discrete, strong, decisive, and capable of taking charge. He was courteous to young Gangulf who would perhaps become a worthwhile man in spite of his chosen profession when by his bearing and manners he could just as well have been in the military. He was not interested in the ex-prima donna or her daughter and saw them rarely, only from a distance during meals, or in the other woman, who had a store or something in the elegant part of Morgenröte Street but who occupied the worst room of the house, with a window to the garden to be sure, but the smallest one, the farthest up, like a servant's or governess's room and thus, by the General's calculations, the cheapest. He said good morning and good evening to the service personnel and did not react rudely if the girl who cleaned his room took it upon herself to speak to him; he did not need to greet the cook because he never saw her; he had seen her only once, a week before moving there, on the day he had gone to see the boarding house on Scheller Street on the advice of his student's mother when they had beaten Bazaine's troops, when he had asked to be shown the kitchen: but he had not greeted her that day since he still did not live in the house.

The day Madame Nashiru arrived was one of many for the General: the almanac indicated a day, and afterwards, insignificantly, he did not know exactly which one in September of 1902; but on that day and precisely that day he had noticed the first chill of autumn, which was useful information only for the choice of clothing. After breakfast he left more warmly clad for the morning and made his way to the museum's library where Mr. Kämpfer had ready the atlas, two treatises on strategy, one by Bonastruc de Porta and one by Watling, and the second volume of *The Compendium of Famous Battles,* subtitled *Modern Wars.* He went to the desk to the right that was tacitly reserved for him and there spread out the maps, opened the book by Watling and went to war thinking as he had thought on other afternoons like that one that he had not fallen into the trap of superficiality because of books like the ones by Knoche and Watling and protocols like the one about the war that Kao Lieu Tchiyueng had embarked upon against the Tartars. He did not return for tea at the boarding house on Scheller Street and only left the library when closing time was announced. Then he abandoned the books, put the notes he had taken into the left pocket of his coat, said good evening, and left.

The General always moved his bowels between twenty minutes and a half hour after lunch and bathed in the afternoons, before the evening meal: not only was it the time when no one else wanted the bathroom, most of all his neighbor on that floor who was usually occupied with his little dolls, and neither would the foreign guest, who had a bath just for herself in her suite, which seemed quite convenient because nothing would have been more disagreeable than to have to use the same sanitary services as a woman, even worse in this case because it involved a woman of another race; in addition it was more healthy to bathe at that hour than in the morning, it predisposed one for sleep, cleansed the skin and removed all the floating grime that the body had accumulated during the day, and returned muscle tone lost during inevitable periods of inaction during daily life; it was an advantage to be able to put on proper clean clothing for the evening dinner, and it gave one the sense of freshness and agility needed to end the day as it had begun. That afternoon he submerged himself in barely warm water and let the cold water run until he was wrapped motionless in an icy block that firmed his flesh and clenched his jaw. He remained stretched out, only his head above water, unmoving, forcing his body to accept the biting cold until it was defeated, counting the seconds like a prayer, imagining ice walls melting around him. When the cold ceased to exist and victorious blood thumped in his neck, wrists, temples, and stomach, he arose, soaped up, and rubbed down with a horsehair cloth. He submerged himself again to remove the soap, left, toweled himself dry, and began to dress. He arrived at the salon a minute before the serving girl lit the lights in the dining room and Madame Helena invited the guests to enter, and there he saw the foreign woman for the first time.

9. Wulda

No needles, ever; Wulda always wished they would order her to do anything besides sewing or mending, because the needles always jabbed her skin and she could not stop staring at the little round drop of blood that formed on the tip of her finger like dew, hard and thick as the tears of the Madonna of the Swords, and she preferred any other kind of work to patching, overcasting or felling seams, or sinking a blunt needle into roasts to enclose the filling, farther from the edge, farther, farther, deeper because the filling will swell and tear it open, ham and nuts soaked in wine and prunes even more and most of all bread moistened with milk and scented with essence of honey; that was why now at the time of day so bright that no one even thought about ordering the lamps lit, she was cleaning ashes from hearths and she understood it: if there is a thick layer of ash over a hidden fire, the flames cannot rise like a tongue, or a finger passing through snow or thick wool, or a leaf through dead overgrowth, but not like soil because soil is wet and soft and the buried shoot manages to poke out, but ashes are dry and fire is only air. Wulda was slowly brushing ashes and collecting the whitish dust in a cardboard box that Lola had stuck the lid on and opened one of the smaller ends with a sharp knife, when she heard the doorknocker strike one, two, three times, and at the third she stood on the tips of her shoes to see who had called and of course saw no one because that person, most certainly the coachman, stood in front of the door, which was in the same outer wall as the window at Madame Helena's desk, but instead she managed to see a woman dressed in mustard yellow with buttons like beetles, a brown hat with tulle, and hidden hands who descended from the coach, took three steps, paused, looked down the street both ways and then for a long long time at the facade of the house. Wulda knew that the woman did not see her. Whenever Wulda thought, she lowered her eyes or looked away so the person with her could not tell what she was thinking from her eyes. But the woman who came toward the house dressed in mustard yellow with buttons like beetles did not see her, and Wulda could think without looking away that she was ugly, something about her was disturbing and it must be that she had come to do harm: this is a sin, Wulda, her Aunt Bauma would say, it is a sin to think badly about people because each one is as God made them and you have to get to know a person and then accept them as they are without judgment, do not judge, Wulda, because he who judges shall be judged; but all this did not matter to Wulda because Aunt Bauma always told her what she should not do instead of what she should do, which Lola and Madame Helena did, and besides a little fear never hurt. She knelt, brushed the dusty ashes together and swept them inside the box, the embers reviving so that at night when it was colder they would grow into fingers and feathers, tongues and leaves; she stood up, covered the hole in the cardboard box with the back of the brush, and crossed the hall to clean the hearths in the salon and dining room. Katja had opened the door to the street and Madame Helena had come down the stairway and the woman who entered extended a hand no longer hidden but covered with a brown glove and they greeted each other. Wulda entered the salon and looked at her own hands: fingers whitish and dry, ashes beneath her nails and on the tips of her fingers and the palms, not black like when she carried coal nor as clean as she had hoped; she walked past the curved wall of the staircase toward the hearth in the salon.

Wulda lived with Aunt Bauma, who cared for her and her sick mother. Aunt Bauma made molds for hats and sold them to the best stores in the city: she said they paid her well because she was the only one who made molds for both ladies and gentlemen in the entire region. The others, and there had been others, had grown tired, had not known how to be patient and earn a reputation through sacrifice and attract clients, and as a result only she was left and could raise her prices and proudly say take it or leave it, and they knew they could not make hats if they did not have good molds. Wulda's mother did not take care of her because she was sick, always bedridden except for a few days in summer when she could sit in a chair next to the window. Aunt Bauma did not let Wulda get near the ill woman because she might be contagious and she had even moved her bed far away to the wall near the door, but Wulda never felt much like getting near her anyway because there were things about the ill woman she did not like: her smell; the shiny skin that seemed about to break apart, probably not like jabbing a finger with a needle and suspecting that the round drop of blood hid deep bodily secrets and dangers, instead a roaring furrow would open that she would be guilty of and could not forget; the noise of air almost like a storm through reeds when it entered her nose, whirled around dirty in the sick woman's chest, and came out; the throat that was always shaking and the eyelids that sometimes rose, did her mothers' open like the eyelids of the new madame? Wulda's mother had dark eyes like Wulda who never let them be seen, but her mother did, and Wulda seemed to see her thoughts like eels, snails, blind fish at the bottom of the sea, the eyes of the poor, poor sick little woman as young Gangulf would say, but surely the thoughts of the woman who had just arrived could not be seen through her eyes tight like grooves in the flooring or cracks in the wall. Wulda had not told Madame Helena about the things her mother had in her chest that her Aunt Bauma talked about, but she had told Mr. Gangulf Rücker who was so handsome and smiled at her and asked about her mother. There had been much less ash in the hearth in the dining room than in the other hearths in the house. When she entered the hallway Madame Helena was taking the new lady toward the back part of the house, to the large suite where Wulda had helped Katja turn over the mattress and move the furniture to clean under the rugs, around the baseboards, and in the corners. With the back of the brush, she covered the hole in the box where the ashes went and carried it down to the kitchen, hoping to see Katja to ask her about the new lady, how she was close up, how she spoke, what she had said, but Katja was not there. Lola was there and told her to put that down, that she was going to set aside the ashes to clean the silverware, and to go back upstairs where she had come from to help Katja, who could not carry all Madame Nashiru's luggage from the vestibule to the large suite, girl don't stand there with your mouth open because open mouths don't make girls prettier and you can get hooked like a fish, hurry, hurry, upstairs, go on, and Lola clapped her hands like she was frightening away evil spirits and while she clapped and cast them out, she laughed. Wulda handed her the box and left, running as Lola had wanted, imagining Lola meeting Aunt Bauma, and would she want to meet her, no, she would not because if they met they would look each other up and down and would not want to talk to each other, they would turn their backs, good-bye madame, do not bother to continue, what have you been saying to the girl standing there as if she were stupid, Lola with her spoon, Aunt Bauma with her spatula, and neither of the two would bother to push in the needle to sew the meat or the edge of the canvas before it dried out. Lola kept the large needle in a little box in the larder, and Aunt Bauma always had five or six needles stuck in the bias at

her neckline. Wulda watched the needles gleam when Aunt Bauma
spoke about hell, but Lola spoke about what men liked and distant
countries where everyone was brown, ran their fingers through their
mustaches, gazed and smiled at you and you were lost, especially
when their deep voices sang oh love my love you must come with
me, why are you lost? Lost like those who were going to hell? But
Aunt Bauma also spoke about the Dormition of the Virgin, and so
she supposed those things Katja told her about the shadows and air
were Katja's visions. Everyone told Wulda so much and she rarely
spoke, she bent down and with great effort picked up the biggest
suitcase: picked it up and put it down, walked and stopped to rest,
and carried it to the large suite that she had helped air out and clean
and in which that very morning she had lit the fire in the hearth
very early, now ash-filled because it had been locked shut until then
and she had not been able to enter with the box and the brush, but
it was open, light shining in everywhere, and the two ladies were
conversing.

10. Deaths

That day like other days, she usually did not bother to imagine fire, rushing to get ready; although imaginary fire turned out delightful, so good she could pause and contemplate it almost adoringly and with anticipation, linger at some sweet bit, repeat it, and watch that contorted tubby body swaying, singing, and turning into a gleaming gem shining with heavenly light, a vision of a chanting siren; but she could not neglect the necessary precise thought, the obligation to leave nothing ill-conceived in the deepest depths, no little detail contingent on what would come next, a falling puzzle piece guided by the force of gravity and the power of miracle into place so everything could be a different life and not this error-filled one, as if what could happen might actually happen; so she could see and hear her on fire and attempting to flee, the world filled with the sound and smell of burning flesh; she would be the only spectator to the dark and shrunken figure emitting puffs of air and black fluids, soul and bile, sound and blood, until her skin was empty. How fine were fires, how very fine, how comforting, but how much work they were, how much organization, and she had to pay attention on that day like other days; she refused to feel ashamed, to become a rodent, a patient larva that dug a perfect tunnel in order to live.

Madame Sophie wanted to know why that girl had not come with the tea, so she answered her for the fourth or fifth time or hundredth, for the thousandth time, for her entire life, that it was not time yet, be patient, while she decided against fire and reconsidered the gallows: to hang her was also a soothing thought although not at all easy to accomplish, not something for today or tomorrow since she was unaccustomed to having a bowline or towline placed over her head, but wit overcomes hurdles and it was not as bothersome as imagining flames; find a way to tilt her head down, drop like a nervous bird that searches and rummages in the dung for a worm and rises up unready, suddenly in the wrong direction with a knot placed on her neck where those chubby arms could not reach since they hardly moved, could not reach the back of her neck at all, which is why she combed her hair and combed and combed it again because she never liked it the first time, and hand mirrors were useless to assure her that she was tidy and no hair, no sparse dry dyed and re-dyed hair held in place by wigs and hats and diadems was loose or out of place. Her bun; she had to spend a lot of time arranging her bun. The house could not be said to have a library and much less their own rooms, although they overflowed with musical scores and albums and magazines about theater and fashion that were of no use to her; but downstairs everything was so precise that if she were to make a little hole in the upper floor and pull up the floorboards and break the framework and kick through the plaster, she would fall into Madame Helena's office, and there was a bookcase whose folding glass doors had beveled edges, bronze pommels, and a plaque on the side for Thompson & Co. London-Paris: travelogues, an encyclopedia, a *Household Administration*, a *First Aid Manual for Accidents, Injuries and Acute Illnesses*, a *Vie des Saints*, and a few other books she never remembered, not even the titles, and in the sixth volume of the encyclopedia between knoll and knowledge, a foldout sheet, not in color like the one for flags or insects but in black and white, displaying knots, each with an explanation of how to tie it and untie it, square knot, overhand knot, slipknot, figure-eight knot, diamond hitch, sheet bend, eye splice, midshipman's hitch, noose, fisherman's knot, surgeon's knot, bowline, all the knots of the world, and the rivers with their islands and the seas with their ports and the cities, all so easy to learn, all slipknots. Once Desdemona finally had the noose around her neck, she could savor the moment. She held her breath and waited for the Moor to enter; or better yet, no, how many times had error or accident struck, no, not the Moor who only pretended to strangle her with his hands, no, not at all, because the public intervened, the hated and beloved public applauded and shouted bravo, and dead Desdemona smiled—and it all collapsed, shattered, rubble, dry, rusty, dusty—no, not Desdemona or Carmen or Violeta or Gilda or Aïda or Floria Tosca or Salome despite his head on a platter; what if she brought her head on a platter instead of the prophet's, if Katja were to come upstairs very serious and composed bringing her gape-mouthed head displaying its false teeth, neck edged with dried blood, eyes open? Yes, oh yes, wide open looking at her with fear, incredulously surprised, if Katja were to leave the platter on the table and leave, discretely, without slamming the door as she left, she would laugh, she would laugh so much and so hard that everyone would come to ask her what had happened, the idiot in the room across the hall and the dead little fly-woman at the end of the hall and even the General and the old man with the toys would come running upstairs and she would tell them that nothing had happened, that she was happy, that was all, and she would close the door and keep laughing with that head of hers on a platter on the table. Perhaps the new guest would come upstairs, the foreigner who had just arrived, but she would not even look at her: foreign women were fine on stage yet awful in real life for a decent person like herself. But when she was in a hurry or when Madame Sophie got too troublesome that day like other days, amid pillows and pictures, tea by the drop or sips and different shoes and shawls, fast as lightning she could always take refuge in a medical error: help, please, a heart attack, my mother is dying, call a doctor, commotion, those useless women who knew nothing except how to make trouble, and finally someone went to look for a doctor and returned with a young one with hardly any experience or an old one whose hands shook or perhaps that stupid boy in the room across the hall who studied medicine, no, not medicine? no, something else, what was he studying? and the pallid doctor would say it's an emergency and pull out a syringe, a needle, break a glass ampule, alcohol, quickly shake the syringe, is about to inject, injects, a little drop of blood and then a tremble, a groan, a shiver, and it is over. She was not interested in what happened to the imbecile or the doctor but she would gaze long at the cadaver, white, mountainlike, finally quiet, forever, eternal, heavy, a wineskin, a block, a cup of iniquity, a spider nest, a bag of garbage, and she would keep looking at it there. How many prayers the dead little fly-woman would say and Katja would bring her coffee and that Helena woman would push her off to the side and take charge of everything, and she herself would leave. She would go to live in Berlin or Paris or Saint Petersburg. She would go to America where a rich heiress like herself could marry a rich ranch-owner right away and go to live in a white palace in the middle of the pampas, served by Indian slaves and visited by other ranchers. He would be named Leonides because he would be like a lion and she would sleep until midday rocked by the wind in the palm trees and the sweet song of the macaws and the far-off roar of the rapids. Her husband would go out to the fields to oversee the farm laborers and one day one of them, crazed by the broiling sun and liquor, seeing him so handsome and fine in his white linen suit and pith helmet and gold spurs, would leap at him to slit his throat with a machete but as fast as a lightning bolt he would pull out his revolver and in midair as he jumped put a bullet between his eyes. She would know nothing of this, would continue sleeping until the servant girls entered, brown, barefoot, with wide lace-edged skirts, necklaces of jaguar teeth, and braids wrapped around their heads, who told her the bath was ready, and she would sink into the water and drink sweet colorful fruit juices from golden bunches of grapes or dark figs or sap from twisted trees gray in the shadow of the forest. At night Leonides, with bright eyes and long copper-colored untidy hair, would play the guitar while grease from mutton sizzled in the fires and guests drank red wine and danced on the lawn: she would sit on the lower terrace beneath a waxed paper parasol that would protect her from the dew and greet arrivals and ask for a song, that pretty one, the one about insupportable absence.

Out of curiosity to see the new guest, Madame Sophie had said that on that day for certain, like other days, they would go down to the dining room at night, and on one of those other nights that Helena woman had assured them that in an instant, in less than an instant, a drowning man sees his entire life, all of it, everything he lived, complete, eloquently recalled, clean and brilliant, what had happened day after day hour after hour in less than an instant, less, even less, far from time, confusing it with death; and that night, that very night, she had started imagining a stumble, a fall, and even a shipwreck, depending on the time available in her room between one whim and another and going to bed, provided she fell from a trans-Atlantic vessel or the boat overturned or she fell off a cliff, so she sank and returned to the surface, breathing a little air, a little, and water, and swallowing and waving her hands, sinking again and coming back up and sinking and coming up again, hardly floating and sinking and seeing her life and never coming up again, sinking to the farthest depths. What she liked about the sea was the green silence, solitude, but not the impossibility that someone, something might come to save her. And she would go to Berlin, to the Americas, all around the world, the deserts, wild plains, lagoons, summits, and jungles.

Of all the deaths, including murder by icepick or meat grinder but never a bullet which was fast although the first-aid manual detailed the ravages of a bullet in the stomach, including a crazed ax murderer or being crushed by a landslide, perhaps the most perfect was asphyxia, although this depended on her state of mind, not just because it was slow and acceptably tragic but because until the end there was hope: someone would come, someone would open the room, someone would have a second thought and remember that she was there; except that no one ever came or did come but too late. In the Americas there were assassins with icepicks and hundred-story buildings you could fall from or from which someone could fall on you, and in the Americas rich people had giant safes that could hold one or two or even three people, with hermetically sealed doors that could not be opened with blowtorches, chainsaws, or cannons, and the sounds of voices or shouts or noise could not pass through the door either. She counted her money only in that room, and the door silently closed behind her because it had a hydraulic mechanism that worked if someone forgot and left the door open, and she did not even notice and kept counting and counting, so much money to count, and only when the air began to run out did she turn around and realize that she was locked in and was going to die there, a prisoner with her money, the bills, the gold coins that suddenly fell from her hands for the last time, and rather than look at them she pounded, she shouted, she sweated, she rolled on the floor crying out, sure that someone would come but no one heard her, she tore at her throat, she pulled out her hair, she ripped off her clothes, she wept, and she died, no, not yet, she was about to die, just about but she opened her mouth seeking air air and everything was hot and opaque around her: there was no more air. One more try, another, and another weak try, and she died.

The idea just occurred to Madame Sophie that perhaps Katja had forgotten or had become ill. Ill? At night in her tiny room with the tiny round window, in her bed pushed against the wall to make space for a chair where she could put the clothes she took off, Nehala had seen the irony of another dream in which she was sick, soothed, and rocked: cool hands, a balcony, broths and creams, cologne on her temples, sunshine. Madame Sophie asked if she thought about doing anything when Katja's footsteps sounded in the hall.

II. "Miraflora"

On the day when Madame Nashiru arrived at the boarding house on Scheller Street, with a little music, a light step, a narrow waist beneath lace trim, underskirt, petticoat and skirt and over that against the cold a tight blue suit blue beret blue ankle boots, Madame Esther sang almost silently to herself returning home happy in the afternoon, imagining itineraries through the darkening city almost as a dance, as exploration and surprise, better yet as an enigmatic path, a backstep instead of a river, a turn, a deceptive pas-de-deux, trois, quatre, foule, a crowd, the more people the better starting with the murmur of discrete voices, Madame? Sir? that filled the salon at "Miraflora" in the elegant business neighborhood on the wide airy street opposite the offices of *Geschrei*. Miss Esther Zaira Schleuster, hidden in a profusion of flowers, concealed and stealthy, lady of the blooms, observant and respectful, walked through the late afternoon city with shadows of eaves and architraves against imposts and archivolts at the doors of potters and cabinetmakers, of seamstresses and necklace beaders down Olmuz Street toward the riverbank; she would have preferred being solitary, mistress of her own savings, life, and will, to be a painter, courtesan, governess, thief, perhaps an actress or lion tamer: she would have been sketched as a portrait of a silent woman in shadowy golden light, eyes half-closed, dyed jet-black hair tied in a chignon at the back of her neck, decorated with a spray of chrysanthemums in a landscape of gray rainy lake country; she would have ridden in a luxurious coach with the curtains raised to let in the sun and would have seen the back of the faint empty silhouette slipping through the doors into the house on Scheller Street and forgotten it in less than an instant, immediately, with a surprising change in posture or expression; she would have arrived at the New World in a caravel and would have gone on to live majestically and cautiously in the golden palaces of Alagoas and Oruro, where servants with dark skin and almond eyes and earrings of bone and silver would shut the curtains tight at midday and would have leaned at the waist over wooden balustrades to see His Majesty's horsemen; she would have jumped like a tiger or the wind or a falling stone on a woman leaving a coach who distractedly held herself in the doorway with a foot still in the air, would have surprised, assailed, robbed her, taken her purse, pearl necklace and earrings, would have pushed her and fled at her shout, losing herself in the crowd, because someone was waiting for her alone in an alley, at a crossroad, an avenue, she would have recited

I met a lady in the meads,
Full beautiful—a faery's child,
Her hair was long, her foot was light
And her eyes were wild

on a stage blinded by the white light so she could not see the abyss of faces and eyes impertinently fixed on her, their binoculars, cigarette cases, jewelry, two thousand hearts, air confined by corduroy and camphor; she would have hunted ferocious animals in the jungle, the king vulture with a crown of feathers like diamonds that laid five brown eggs that smelled of civet on mountain peaks, or silky tigers or the Dramanabad panther; she would have had scratches, scars, and bruises, an injured and rigid hand but eyes like beasts; she would not live in the boarding house on Scheller Street, which was a pity, she liked the house, but would have lived in an attic apartment with glass roofs and the scent of turpentine along the top of a very old building at the end of a narrow little street; in Gefte Street traversed by closed coaches and inhabited by women who wore Damascene halters with rubies like boulders from Afghanistan, facing the Main Square and the palace with its shades always drawn; here and there looking back over her shoulder; near the Classical Theater in a mansion in Hundszunge Street, where it was said Friedrich Schröder lived with Sofia and Guellermina during the entire 1807 opera season; in a green-painted covered wagon with yellow trim and bright red flowers over its little windows.

She walked slower when she saw the dark line of park trees far away: if she kept walking at that speed, with a little music in her throat and fast feet, she would arrive too early, meet no one, enter the doorway alone and climb the stairs alone, walk down the corridor, pass the first door without turning her head, looking straight ahead at the second, turn right impassive and autocratic, and just few steps ahead would see her own door. She would already have her key in hand, and perhaps she would have taken off the beret and then would hear with what pleasure the lock mechanism move, shift, slip, open, the door swinging toward the shadows inside, lamps waiting in the blurry light, hardy any light entering from the garden through the window. Her room was above the suite of that new guest she had heard about but had not seen, although her own room was not as big or complete; it was no suite with a salon, bedroom, and bath, two hearths and doors to the garden. Hers was a little less than the size of the bedroom downstairs but likewise had a window to the garden. And it had another window to the hall and a third, smaller one to the air shaft where young Gangulf's window opened along with the window in the corridor that passed alongside the empty room in the front. One floor down, Mr. Pallud's false balcony faced this air shaft, and a window of the large suite at the end of the corridor, and a window of the dining room. If she looked out of it, which she did not and only out of the one facing the garden, she could have seen the back of a chair in the dining room; the lower shelf of the case almost like a shop window where Mr. Pallud kept his miniature toys; a painting that hung on the wall of the corridor next to the vacant room by Ziem of lilacs in a vase at a window through which could be seen a summer landscape in a complete contradiction because blue, lilac, violet were colors for winter flowers, according to Mr. Celsus; and a portion, hardly any of young Gangulf's room, an armchair, the corner of a wall and the jamb of one of the doors, because his room was the only one that had two doors; she would see no more because even leaning into the air she could not have seen inside the lower suite. Madame Esther did not ever lean out of that window and preferred the window to the garden because she liked trees, plants, paths, and no one else's window facing hers. Someday, not in caravels which was a daydream but in a trans-Atlantic ship, she would go to live in a country in the Americas where she could lean out of the window and see infinite green, the untempered yellow of the sun, the gray of sea mist, the reddish sunset, the interminable white salt marshes, or the leaden, granite-gray sea. Her father had talked and talked on long afternoons, hurried mornings, after mass in sunny walks, on sleepless nights, and even as he evaded the face of death, about leaving like his brother Manfred to go to those countries with jungles, flocks, swarms, herds, estates without end, cities that grew swallowing up prairies and estuaries, to make his home in the countryside amid a settlement of compatriots between two rivers or in a neighborhood that would reproduce the streets of his childhood, buy a machine on credit, two if he could, open a printing shop and, if God willed, later buy a house with the earnings, set up another business, marry off his daughter, grow tanned under the sun, smell of ink, stain his fingers, trim his mustache, take afternoon walks with his hands in his pockets, and sit in a café beneath the shelter of trees from which yellow pollen and transparent petals drifted down, with long-tailed birds high in the sky, large godlike night cats keeping watch from roofs, and devilish guitar players, loud and fast. Madame Esther never wondered about the names of flowers, had treasured her father's face but not her mother's whom she never knew, and had also kept the music, the beat, the rhythm of an ocarina or xylophone, a cadence, symmetry, a metric of words and movements that she could not awaken with a piano or violin but she reconciled with time, in which time was a wave, arms that rocked her, a name and resonance in the most enigmatic moment of time, sheltered by Lola's almost physical wisdom or Katja's shadows, like the light on the pearls around the neck of the woman who had just arrived at the house on Scheller Street. Very slowly she neared the corner, turned, and managed to see him on the unlit street, and, so he would see her, she raised her hands to take off her beret, touch her hair, pat it, smooth it a little, affirmed and protected in this part of the world. Young Gangulf stepped aside with a smile so she could enter ahead of him: in the vestibule, the lamp next to the mirror winked, vibrated, exploded, and rose to the heavens, and there shone for ten thousand years, and the applause and the whistles deafened her, skewered her with needles of ice, platinum, mint, and snow in her throat and deep inside, and she said good evening and thank you as she took off her gloves and opened the chancel door to the corridor. Young Gangulf also said good evening: "The new concept of man's difficulties now places us high above useless metaphysical speculations. Nowadays attention, observation, and analysis of material deeds as dispassionately and objectively as possible are the inevitable preparation that must precede all careful investigation. The scientific approximation of intellectual activity convinces us that in the intimate correlation of chemical processes is found the secret of thought at whose doors the naive scholars of the past knocked without response." The warrior in this expedition that is life, the exploration of the minimal to reach the superlative, young Gangulf thought, is not the one who fights battles but he who lives peace like war, rest like attack, obscurity like rescue, indifference like passion, he who is not defeated, he who cannot be vanquished. Madame Esther said that the first chills were in the air and young Gangulf agreed but added that he preferred this weather because it was easier to concentrate on his studies in his room than with the windows open in summer. She agreed in front of the door to his room but he continued: he asked if she would permit him to accompany her and open her door, and she, taking a clumsy step but not quite tripping, squeezing to the key before giving it to him, almost reaching again to take off her beret, just said yes, that was very kind of him.

12. Invitation and Conjure

If she had her way, that dining room would be open and lit every day and every moment, all the time, table set, fire all sparks and spikes, all flame and kindling, heat and light but not in summer, for summer was the time to close the curtains to block the sun and open the north windows, and people passing on Scheller Street would see without meaning to look knowing they should not but the window was so near their eyes, and looking in they would be astonished at the crystal and china, potbellied fruit, sumptuous bottles, festive silvery mirror, a carnival on the mantlepiece over the fireplace. Open as it should be, not like an office or bedroom, much less a bathroom or dressing room; open like a church, invitation and conjure at any time, confusion of lunches and breakfasts, melon and chocolate, dinners, teas and aperitifs, toasts, petit-fours, honey and sabbath stew, spicy breaded chicken and molasses, people entering and leaving and greeting each other and pulling out chairs, a muddle of scents, jumble of voices, the last lights put out in the house, the first ones lit, Katja next to the sideboard, Wulda in the basement decanting wines, Lola dreaming, a dream of wrapping herself in the entrails of the earth rocked by secret lianas stronger than branches, soft, warm, savory, a dream of crouching and suckling, her immense body agile, rising brilliant to the surface, moons like pearls, dreams of seeing wheat, of the creeper she was going to plant, of a city, not this one, with towers and minarets next to jungles where the climbing vines curved away and the water in the drain spun to the other side and the sun made another trip over yellow land awoken by the pampas wind. Whether kneading, cutting, dicing, beating, or sauteing, whether sifting or marinating, whether whisking or juicing, Wulda watching everything attentively and Katja coming downstairs dressed in black and white, with her hair in a bun and silent shoes; whether toasting or poaching, whether she serves, covers, sprinkles, whatever she does, the platters are filled with colors, vales, and patterns, of tenderness in shadows or peaks, and they steam and go, leaving a barely visible track going up the stairs, an acrid fog, a heavy veil against the nose, and the scents hurry upstairs and elbow their way to the table leaving Lola behind, abandoned, all the work and troubles mitigated, moving away from the stove with a sigh and an order to Wulda to serve the sauce in a sauce boat, the hake without breaking it apart while lifting it out with a slotted spoon, and the vegetables, girl, bathed in sauce but the whole nuts on the fish and a glass of that wine.

While Lola eats, the first to come to the salon that night was Mr. Ethan Pallud dressed in gray, the high collar of his white shirt cutting into his skin, the very blue gaze of his eyes erratically taking in things and shadows of things without stopping, a book in his right hand, leaving his room behind with its echo of whimpers of cushions and velvet, faint clicks of gears, pillows, axles, tiny pendula, wheels, and levers; passing the landing of the staircase and entering the salon but first pausing for a second at the closed door of Madame Helena's office without looking at it. Katja now in the salon, motionless and alert, did not hear words and sentences not meant for her but at his arrival she receded before he came and saw her, returned to the dining room she had just left, closed the doors and paused in the shadow among the solemn backs of the chairs, in the orbit of the aromas waiting on the platters that were already on the sideboard each in a covered dish, embers in the grate for warmth, fruit and cream on the lower shelf, wines on the ledge: she did not want him to see her, did not want him to call her on the pretext of asking what was on the menu or telling her when she should come the next day to clean his room. She wished someone else would come soon because the penumbra, the penury, the puff of time brought her voices of beings and silhouettes of voices; wished for anyone to come, not Madame Helena who always waited for the others to arrive before she entered, but someone, the new lady who might have hurried because she did not know the customs of the house and did not want to be late, even the General, someone, if there were two she could leave, latent, lance, lash, leave the dark dining room, pause at the double glass doors, wait without being troubled by winged beings or men with windblown capes or top hats that scaled mountains, if only it were time to open the doors, light the lamps, display the shining china and crystal. Madame Helena? No, no one, the shadow of someone or something or the old man with the toys walking in the salon, his pointed nose cutting through the air, silky claws and pointed teeth, grey, bluish, transparent, a box in his chest and a shelf in his belly with birds, giraffes, harpsichord players, dolls who spoke with die-cast jaws held with pins to their painted little tin faces, toys on shelves where they lie and peck, bite and die; from reading so much while everyone else slept he knew what girls fear, what the wind drags in, what the water carries. The world of shadows affected Katja but did not dazzle her, she met it on the way, on that very day that had now passed and the house was solid once again, changed but solid, perhaps not indifferent but silent and firmly serious, and in the darkness of the dining room she could see how cherry trees blossomed, how they fell, how almond tree flowers opened at any time of the year, how they withered into ochre and cadmium, she could hear how the roots of all the trees in the world moaned. Katja had been born near Klumbach in a farmhouse that flooded in autumn when the river rose, was dry and windy in summer when the earth spoke, and Luduv had taught her how to hear it. Luduv had died but sometimes he returned, and that night Katja felt he was going to come out of the shadows, appear from behind a seat, arise next to the sideboard, spy through the curtains luminous as the sun, with his sweet-sour caress as he passed, and at that moment two people entered the salon, mother and daughter, and Katja opened the door, left the dining room, stepped far to the right, hands clasped as Madame Helena had taught her, to wait until it was time.

The General heard those steps but they seemed to be nothing, a rubbing, brushing, imaginary rain, forgotten sand, not his neighbor in the room opposite and especially not the service women, and without needing to look at his watch he resumed combing his hair in no hurry, adjusted his tie, examined the crease in his slacks, checked his pockets, looked around to be sure everything was in place, neared the door; and at that moment he did hear steps but they were going down the stairway almost tumbling: the young student from the upper floor.

Young Gangulf greeted the room all around when he entered the salon, asked about the health of Madame Simeoni and whether Miss Nehala had enjoyed her day, and went to the chair where Madame Nashiru had just sat down, when Madame Helena entered. Today, Katja thought, will I have to open the doors of the dining room sooner than usual? But no, Madame Helena would open them as always at the exact time: she said she would like to introduce the new guest in the house and just then the General entered, and as Madame Helena presented everyone with few gestures and hardly a step back, Miss Esther entered. Katja liked Miss Esther, whose smile was not distant or tight and especially not twisted like the old man with the toys; she did not know about the General because he never smiled; and the fat women would giggle dryly and cover their mouths with the tips of their fingers. Madame Helena approached Madame Nashiru, who stood up and smiled. Madame Helena was dressed in a long flared black dress with a vermillion satin sash at the waist. Madame Nashiru wore sky blue, a dress of a fabric that seemed to be darker in the folds and the hem, and a pearl necklace and pearls in her earrings and rings: Luduv had told her one afternoon, she was not sure if it was in winter or summer, that she had to fish for shadows the way they fished for pearls, to dive, dive down, and find them; pull them from their fleshy stalks and bring them up. Katja had not known until then that pearls were fished: she thought they were animal eyes or came out of the ground or sprouted from rocks or were made by chemists. She thought that Madame Nashiru must have fishermen at her service, pearls, so many pearls: she must have a cook and maid, lady in waiting and coachman and errand boy and fishermen. Miss Esther did not have pearls, only a gold chain around her neck and blue eyes below hair a bit mussed; a brown skirt and white blouse with cuff and collar embroidered in brown and gold. Katja did not care how the fat women were dressed but she watched them as they greeted Madame Nashiru and told herself that no matter how close the shadows came, she would never squint her eyes or frown like that when she greeted someone, when she said good-bye, when she had to talk to a lady she did not know, never. It was time, and it seemed to Katja that everyone was talking all at the same time except the General: something had happened to him, he was not standing rigid like the back of a chair but bent forward, one shoulder higher than the other, his face shining like the pearls that she had seen and he could not stop looking at. Madame Helena spoke to everyone and no one specifically, gesturing only with her eyes, her large-toothed mouth, the turn of her head like a colossus half buried in the sand or a miniature in a glass case Katja remembered from cleaning at a different house, her voice deliberate and error-free with meaning on the wing, as the fat mother would say who was born with songs in her mouth. She said that Madame Nashiru had arrived from Tokyo, so very interesting, and was going to remain six months or at least until a business was established and underway that she would open on Kafter Street, until the personnel had come from her country and she had contracted staff from within the city. A jewelry store, she added, and young Gangulf in a decorative attack one-on-one with the elements that the General would have admired if he had not become perversely attracted by what he feared most, spread one of his smiles around the room and followed it by saying that this would a good idea because there was only one jewelry shop in the city, the one across the street from the tea room of Miss Esther, had she met Miss Esther Schleuster? Everyone stood because it was now time, a habit in their afternoons and evenings, and moved the same way, driven as a group toward a terrible dream that brought liberation and fear: me? jump into a bottomless well? Katja unclasped her hands, turned, and before she reached for the doors she chanced to see everyone on foot except the Simeonis piled on a sofa like bags of rags that someone had forgotten on a worn wooden bench in a station smelling of smoke and rust where people waited and wept, where the next day all the stories would be erased and start again refreshed: bells, whistles, shouts, forgotten bags of rags on a worn wooden bench. The double glass doors with beveled panes where light danced opened smoothly without a sound, and Katja entered the dining room, opened them fully, secured them, lit the lights, stood next to the sideboard, and waited.

The velvety scent of nuts sauteed in butter and boiled in fish broth entered Miss Esther's nose and she felt hunger tightening her waist and throat: gobble down fish, sauce, bread, house, mills, grass, the world; swallow water, sea, and waterfalls, to awaken again on another shore, able to laugh without memories. It was not hunger, it was happiness. Katja brought her the platter and Miss Esther

ANGÉLICA GORODISCHER

served herself a minuscule bit and a spoonful of sauce. She guessed Katja's thoughts: take more, eat more, come on, another piece. She waved her hand and Katja moved on.

The book in his pocket bothered him, everyone laughing, Kati-Kati went to the other side of the table and he did not care, fish, meat, whatever but let dinner end right away, let him return to his room because it annoyed him to leave a page half-written: "Articulated figure sitting on a Queen Anne style chair." Mr. Pallud's skin grew and stretched until it became almost invisible, a sparkle on his temples and fingers and the bottoms of his feet; but a wrinkled excess lining his groin, his armpits and the backs of his knees, knotted into his navel and tamed into his orifices, with thin nose hairs and rough eyebrows over eyes fastened on the waist of Kati-Kati, a silly girl and as quiet as anyone could be. When he traveled, when he explored, when he extended himself over the world's vast floating distant globe, when he left, no more white fish or creamy sauces, instead dark strong meat beneath a copper bronze fiery threatening sun. When he was no longer there but in the confines of the jungle, on the borders of deserts, he would not need books in his pockets, a white linen suit would be the fashion, held in place only by the watch chain around his body, and they would look at him differently, not the way Madame Helena was at that moment: Kati-Kati was offering him the platter and for all that he wanted to take his time, Madame Helena continued to look at him and he had to put down the serving utensils and the silly girl left at the moment when the daughter of the singer was saying that what she most wanted in life was to travel and she listed Paris, London, New York, Tokyo, Buenos Aires, Saint Petersburg. Madame Nashiru smiled. He clenched his silverware; the elastic skin stretched and contracted, stretched and contracted.

Tokyo? Tokyo was a barbaric city twenty years ago when she was there singing *Aïda* but perhaps Madame Nashiru did not understand

68

what Madame Sophie Simeoni had meant to say by barbaric city and that was why she kept smiling. Her daughter wanted to make her be quiet—would she just be quiet with knots, flames, seas, steel blades, behind shut doors or in bed howling, sleeping, trembling? Just be quiet? Round, gray, soft, and voracious, they did not seem to concern themselves with the golden air of the dining room or the other guests or the time or the pearls. They swallowed air, words, food; they squinted, took one mouthful after another, and a shining ring formed around their mouths until the daughter looked at her mother more than the mother looked at her daughter, she gestured at the napkin, and the two wiped their mouths, their fingers sinking into the fabric that wrapped around their chins. Katja came with the bottle of wine. But where they most liked *Aïda*, according to Madame Simeoni, was in Buenos Aires. The lament in the second act had earned ovations and one night in the recently inaugurated Columbus Theater in the presence of the president of the republic, she had to repeat it three times, three.

Madame Helena nodded: she foresaw a new shining aureola, this time of broth forming around Madame Sophie Simeoni's mouth and cream seeping out of the corners of her lips and bonbons sticking to her teeth. She leaned over to tell Madame Nashiru about the fame Madame Simeoni had enjoyed around the world years earlier. She also pointed out her daughter's devotion in caring for her now that her health was in decline and the public, except for a few experts, had forgotten her. The ingratitude and the whalebones in her corset bit Madame Helena's heart: she kept her back straight the way a juggler kept colored balls in the air one over another, like soap bubbles, always about to trick her and slip and escape, straight and upright, an inevitable arc in her viscera and no other concession to softness, buttocks firmly pressed against the chair, shoulders in a straight line parallel to her waist, and eyes everywhere. At some instant, in some corner, at times a whimper might awaken, for which she had to sit even straighter, be obstinate, maintain primacy, any advantage no matter how small over disorder, and block the pain or even the hint of an ache. Madame Helena preferred dessert without cream at the evening meal but since this was a special day, she had ceded to Lola's suggestion. She signaled to Katja: the General's cup was empty again.

Eyes empty, fish swimming in a sea of eyes, everything white including the storms, terminating in a silver platter looking at the ends of the teeth of a fork that was nearing, penetrating, passing through a body that opened obediently: all the soldiers, the entire battalion was one body maintained and contained by one voice, one music, and one order. There in front, empty glass, empty field, and only one more body needed to arrive unstained. Emptiness seemed too much like chaos: the General did not want to confess that in the nothingness between bodies, it was impossible for him to support the order of clothing, accessories, details, and so, with the platter at his side, he had to place his hands over that body, take the serving utensils, render it to pieces the way a battalion fell to pieces before a machine gun, serve himself a slice of meat and return victorious walking over new earth asking himself how it was possible that I, with a useless shield, scuffed boots, tooled leather breastplate tainted with sweat and blood, how have I become the lord of this. Anxious with all his might to be back in his room, in the darkness, to save himself the sight of another mouthful, he obliged himself to swallow, for he had survived far away, exited into emptiness without gender or words, stubborn and bitterly opaque. This woman did not seem like a woman but like an erroneous boy, that smooth body, obedient face, that foreigner, that enemy naked and with her back to him, narrow buttocks beneath that blue dress, could look like a boy, a stable boy, a god without attributes, his soldiers, pearls like bone tears sliding on an open wound, the itinerary of the park at dawn, everything lost contour and sharpness and Madame Helena spoke serenely, terribly, unmistakably, and perfectly in charge of the situation, in the tea ceremony, as women do when they are determined to make everyone else happy.

Young Gangulf never drank tea: the Titans, in his opinion, subsisted on the rocks of time, and he, when he arrived punctually, had chocolate. I prefer the rocky, gray, and firm face of the General like a Herschel plaque to the yellowish face of the old idiot; I don't like the round faces of women; above all I prefer the shrieking roaring face lost in terror. He said as if pirouetting in a thundering circus that all ceremonies are mysterious, battles, communion, prizes, opening nights, is it not so, dear madame?

Downstairs, Lola sighed. Katja measured the wine left in the bottles and wondered whether Wulda was awake or had fallen asleep sitting in a chair low enough for children, her head resting on the white wall, mouth open, hands on her skirt. Sleep, Luduv said, standing in the windowsill, sleep, the snare of sleep.

Part Two: Toni Plays

13. A Tiny Thought

A tiny thought crossed the street like a flash of lightning; it was an orange-hearted blue spark that would have been invisible on a sunny day but that day was going to be gray, all the gray of winter's end, after being white and before being green, gray clouds and blankets on horses, a tiny thought round as a wish crashed against the dry facade when dawn came to Scheller Street. People might be sleeping behind closed windows, behind balconies blind as a mole or chrysalis, bodies might move in spite of themselves imprisoned by hindering blankets or a coat swimming in dark dreams, abandoned and vulnerable; there might be a single sigh made from all the air of all the breaths, mouths might slacken and eyelids tremble, cramps might grip the elderly and terror the children; and the entire sweet night slid toward the smooth river where dawn would come to this part of the world. What had been Mill Alley was still a ravine in the darkness down which flowed women dressed in mauve or sky blue or white, fat Hoenken sniffing the approaching rain, the most enchanting of hosts, servant women with wide hips who carried the change from purchases hidden in their apron pocket, Novalis in search of the primal fire that arises from the center of the earth. A tiny eagerly buoyant thought touched the favored foreheads and flourished in halberds, rockslides, and drumrolls: barely light, the overcast day barely born in cold dispersed the greetings of men, the measured steps of girls, the chatter of servants; morning hardly entered the mouth and ears of the perplexed merchant; softly at first and then louder, filling corridors and antechambers with echoes, the padding footsteps of the nursemaids and wet nurses on the wooden floors of their rooms. Breasts filled with milk ached, fingertips touched lips rough with sleep, hands reached for door handles and towels, the struggle ceased between legs in the folds of eiderdown tossed to the feet of beds, the scent of coffee rose; and with the first voice that established wakefulness, anguish and intrigue reinstated themselves. A tiny sinuous thought like a whim returned from the street to the interiors of the houses, reflected, multiplied, changed into a vision that flooded the eyes and tightened the throats; and mothers sighed and nursemaids knit their brows.

The houses on Scheller Street had moldings, weathervanes, balconies, alcoves, lightning rods, and wide carved polished doors that were varnished once a year. Storms that came from the north struck the facade of Madame Helena's boarding house and her neighbors' but the houses across the street received southern sunlight in winter and the easterly or mountain winds that made the panes in the windows shake. The hallways retained the outside chill, the rooms were wrapped in family intimacy and the smell of soup or tuberose; funeral processions left the doors, prodigal sons returned through them, messengers left, visitors entered hauling pride and errors, trying to hide the ragged ghosts they carried on their waistbands or hatbands, the fatigue, the acid breath of an argument. In contrast, the windows and especially the balconies announced the world: one could open the curtains, lean out, spy, return inside, leave them half-open, and illuminate rooms thanks to them, wait, call someone, secretly observe, and even be surprised. Prudent openings, the windows of the houses on Scheller Street eased themselves awake in the mornings with the flurry of cleaning girls, fulfilled by fringes, rosettes on the cushions, bedspreads, coats, and blankets folded over parapets and bannisters. Hurrying, collars warm, hands in gloves, boots shined, little eyes alert, through the processional doors polished once a year left the daughters and sons; the older ones alone and clumsy, helmet-like hats on their heads, straps across their chests under their coats held books hitting their hips at each step as they ran after someone or pretended to; the smallest ones with a nursemaid or servant; girls with headscarves and caps edged with lace, homework in a bag embroidered with initials; boys with a short hooded cape edged with leather, satchels with books: a tiny thought moved the singing feet, the trail of voices, the greetings of the maids or snubs behind the words, the intention, the haste, a tiny impatient thought evasive as a lie. At that moment Lola sits before the white table and Wulda pours a trickle of cream into a cup of thick chocolate that sinks and is lost, with two toasted marzipan rolls the color of grapes in the sun, dark, translucent, and frosted with pink, crunchy looking and rough to the taste, and she thinks of the mystery of stems, sap in veins, the water that feeds wood, the roots like wise tentacles although she would not use those words: strange things, she says, presences, as if they were little animals that cannot be heard and yet proper Christians, heads held high, saying no, not at all. Her creeper, for example, climbs immoderate and nimble, perhaps overwhelmed by snow and cold, vengeful now that the ice is melting and the river flows agitated and noisy, presumptuous as a rich man and arrogant as a boss, never caring at all for the coming sea, bursting its banks, lanced by yellow light and white fish; the change of season has brought her here and she has never felt like this, her arms useless, an enormous space opening in her head and pushing her palate down, ears out, hair falling from braids and buns while her entire queenly body, stomach and kidneys, belly and bladder, piles into a hardening heap and gives her this appetite, these desires, this impulse, this force that turns like a wheel at the end of the world and consumes itself in mere light, never in labor. At night sleep comes immediately and she stubbornly sleeps a couple of hours but then she suddenly awakes as if obliged to climb the walls of a well where she fell without knowing how or when, and light enters filtered by the shutters as consolation. She herself is like a whim of the plants: there are dishes she liked a year ago that now she will not taste and even dislikes preparing; big meals but without grace or elegance that she would never cook even for Café Netzel, and if she thinks about them they take over her thoughts and dance, making her mouth water until she frightens them away, irritated, ill humored, like the buzzes entering her head through her ears when a storm is coming from far away which at that moment only the body feels and it is time to put screens in the windows to keep out flies trapped in minuscule whirlwinds of dust and dirt. Perhaps she is sick, perhaps in fact death is courting her, perhaps what she needs is a man who will stay at her side a little longer, all her life, a week, two months, until the creeper grows and raps around the frame she has placed on the wall and reaches Miss Esther's window up there and makes her life a little happier. Lola's life is like a decoy, thunder, magic fire, sun on the windowsill: it would be a pity for it to end, if suddenly she were to ask herself but what is happening to me and discovered that she was dead and no more sputtering, no more reaching around to her back to let out her corset, laughing. But that should not be, why should it, who announced it to her, between what columns did she pass where she failed to see the angel of life. Golden marzipan, pink when baked, soft belly, voices of children in the street, thaw and flood, Lola thinks about Sunday and smiles to herself and tells Wulda to eat another roll, one more, she really needs it now that her poor mother has died and she is so sad, as transparent as a soul from holding back so many tears, come on, eat one, come on, one more.

14. Windows

If outside there were iron and bronze
and sometimes porcelain doorknobs, inside there were curtains
and silence, entrenched and almost never placid silence because
there must be speech and almost certainly fury and vengeance,
tempers that ricochet off children like another lofty secret to be
ascertained as they grew into ostentatious gentlemen and haughty
ladies, although they hoped to be svelte horsemen who went
to war and damsels with wreaths of flowers in the parks with
waterspouts, fountains, arbors, cobblestone paths, and murmuring
sounds, which does not mean that silence exists or that it could
be called anything other than absence; curtains still as marble,
silk-like shields, a pretense and defense against the light, buckler
and protection against indecent stares, and above all, vestments.
To put up curtains has been a science since ancient times no less
intricate for being domestic. When Madame Helena renovated
the house on Scheller Street to take in boarders, Mr. Frenzen
showed her workshop tables covered with all variety of poles,
brackets, clasps, rings, tassels, hooks, cornices, pins, swags, overlap
carriers, pulleys, and cords, to say nothing of fabric and cloth, the
wares and textiles he kept pulling out of cabinets and unrolled
from its bolts soft or heavy to the touch, mere ideas, a vision that
she held and had yet to take form, standing because who wants
armchairs and footstools while creating a solid exterior that at the

same time must be friendly, a place one would wish to enter and live. Curtains in the boarding house of Madame Helena and the other houses on Scheller Street disrupt the windows more than they dress them up, some that only serve as veils and through which can be seen the light of a match at night or the shadow of every hero or villain hung on the gallows throughout history; curtains for nursing children and the faded mornings of illness but still luxurious, opulence and splendor to spare, hands that slide through pleats and which hide ever-equal folds and the slippery bodies of the dead who do not return but Luduv himself appears summertime sharp climbing grassy steps, where opaque desires and impassioned tears slide down, where in autumn grain is sown in the fields that imitate the wrinkles of old women, lines from the edge of the nose to the corner of the lips, the cracks of the dry hungry mistreated and still resentful earth that throws its children aside and sends them to serve a gigantic ill-tempered god; enveloped by winds of storm and war, bodies struck down by death's diligent blow, gray creatures from the center of the earth, catastrophe-sized headlines in newspapers, the source of other machines, still others, salt-cellars and violins smashed to bits, unrecognizable picture frames of portraits and perhaps a barely audible moan, a splash of blood fresh from arteries, daily and difficult, an improbable and kindly bud, a breeze, madame, from lost gold. In the salons, dining rooms, libraries, and music rooms, the curtains overlap and overlay each other, they hide and protect, wool, silk, crepe, satin, velvet, golden cords, fringes, straps, and braids held by the inner frame; the brightest bedrooms try to reduce the shadow and dim the day, and children's rooms display curious backlit figures with flutes, tambourines, sensible animals, and landscapes; the bathrooms have leaded or etched glass instead of curtains filling round or oval windows set high up whose only sash pivots and is held open by a hook on the wall with a chain that tarnishes with time; in kitchens the curtains are smooth and easy white cotton; and in the maids' rooms they depend on rank, almost immobile hierarchies: if they exist, they are linen, without pleats, purpose, pampering, and if possible without sin.

15. The Sun

Halfway through the morning, Lola organizes, counts, and rolls out dough, while Katja and Wulda clean, Madame Helena rushes around with hard-backed notebooks where she enters income and expenses and work to do in the house because soon the season will change and it will be spring, while Miss Esther smiles, lit like a relief figure on a frieze by the light that enters the shop window and silhouettes the golden letters edged in black of "Miraflora" on the dark gray rug, because Mr. Celsus tells her quite seriously that it may seem like winter to her but not really, for winter is over. Perhaps it has ended and that gives her this shape and outline; perhaps the curtain will be raised over a parade of feet and hands and faces on the washed surfaces of streets, sidewalks, steep roofs, floors, the curve of all-new porcelain and silk, as if deflowered again, like the chatter of guessing games and charades of children who, while Lola contemplates the platters that have been served, arrive at midday with servants and shouts, pattering shoes and busy hands through the doorway, hungry, hot, thinking about the afternoon that lies ahead when the day is no longer gray but yellow.

Because the sun came out at noon. It came out over a grayish world in a resentful winter and nothing could be done about it: in some houses the curtains were chastely closed because this sun, excessive, out of place and propriety, might fade the tapestries and worse, strike the skin on forearms and behind earlobes of protected and obedient girls inciting their thoughts, girls who transformed in that season like the sun, trading black kid gloves for itchy white lace gloves with tiny round silk-covered buttons at the wrist. The sun struck facades, excited shadows, split on edges, pushed borders; the light gave vigor to large rooms and shine to details on handrails on stairways. Maybe it was warmer, maybe it was not, but many women stopped, aware of themselves, too aware for a second or less, straightened their heads, eyes searching corners as if they might seek and find there the proof of a sacrilege, enchantment, or secret white light could illuminate the lives of everyone they knew and their own lives, the way a kinetoscope's revelation evokes a little childlike noise in a darkened room; and many men disabused themselves of that presumption, the chill over what they had managed to flee without a trace, and frightened it away, amazed by their own strength, sure about the terrain they trod. Nevertheless, small thoughts ripe like grapes and like them in bunches, almost invincible, small wild juicy thoughts roiled like sparks, squatted like buttresses, climbed fiercely, flew bravely, slid down throats and rose up and out like bubbles, and this time mothers smiled and nursemaids cleared their throats.

Which has to do with noise, obviously. Scheller Street held what Mill Alley never did: in the time of the fat merchant when the words of Novalis sang seductively to the intimate heat of bodies and the igneous heat of newly conceived land; when strong square houses were built and contours of dreams were transformed by stone and mortar, the alley harbored all manner of noises, squeals, shouts, blows, yells, whistles, dins, voices, and racket; women called out, men gave orders, children cried, beasts brayed, and cartwheels screeched and struck doorways, bread was kneaded, rugs were beaten, pots broke, and at times songs were sung in the kitchens and at towlines. But then silence came with a century, as if saying there was no reason for delusions, and asking for polish, cleanliness, reserve, and logic instead of vanity, contending that we will all be happy and have houses like these flanked by leafy trees, polished by diligent servants, from which our bedecked coaches will leave toward happiness; who could doubt it, riches, aircraft, dirigibles, dominions, pantelegraphs, all the marvels of life revealed without danger or pain. Silence is absence, heavy and grave, the absence of flesh, flesh and word, word and body, prudent resolve, deliberation, good manners, and the right gloves for every occasion. Madame Helena had tea in her rooms and Sophie Simeoni scolded her daughter ten meters above; the sun took its time, Miss Esther wore white, Mr. Pallud bent over a violin player seven centimeters high and gently brushed the plaid pants of the minuscule figure with his finger, young Gangulf drew circles on a sheet of paper, Madame Nashiru placed the pearls from the most recent shipment onto trays lined with midnight blue velvet or white silk, and, from the street, hidden in a doorway, the General spied on her.

16. The Almost Violet Light

Despite the sun's insistence, day became night as fast as a thief, silently, no corner unexplored, meticulously reconnoiting the territory at first, then faster so it could finish as soon as possible. But for a moment the light wavered on pale surfaces as if it still wanted to reveal and reflect, although it did not last; a very brief moment that no one would have noticed if it had not been precisely the light that made Katja see the sand fall from the garden wall, dissolve in water that erased the wall, leaving a hole without a single trace of anything having been there, showing her how Luduv could not be heard when he spoke quietly, at least with ears: a field of souls sowed with green stones that dissolved in water again, and arms and knives were lifted from the water with screaming, utter conflict, utter lies, utter wisdom from dreams, erosion, and the specter she was loath to see. Except that she was lost, captive of a merciless hand and distant voice: Katja belonged to two worlds and in both she was obliged to do the behest of other people, orders from Madame Helena in one world to which she was expressly indifferent but took pains to complete, and mandates from Luduv in the other world with her consent. As always things happened to her sight and hearing in the indecisive season with evasive winds and sun to evoke Luduv, leaning on a grainy wall or crouching at her side, yet despite this she kept polishing the mother-of-pearl handles of dessert knives with ashes moistened in olive oil: Luduv was saying why should you be afraid, you must go down, down deeper, confident all the way, I am here to help you rise but you have to go down, down, I can do nothing now, open the traps and let out the swarm, does the buzzing frighten you? No, it did not. The fragrant chamois went back and forth under prodigious fingers. Katja's were long and slim, palms wide compared to those girl-like fingers, strong smooth hands, tight in the winter from the cold, unfortunately with split, peeling cuticles at times; Madame Helena wanted the nails cut square and kept clean, and Luduv made them sing, rubbing his own nails on them, like crickets, like cicadas; but fleshy and pink in summer, hands she paid no attention to when she heard sounds and Luduv held her in daydreams. And so the light left its watch and the sea of souls bellowed in a whirlpool and disappeared on the head of a pin. Katja wanted to call him, Luduv! but Wulda was watching. Although she was never sure what Wulda was watching.

Luduv was gone. Splendid was the afternoon voice that had changed, heard in the doorways of stores, on the steps of offices, on high at the seafront, and in the aura of trees that arose without warning; only an occasional cabinetmaker or gardener who cared for wood was tipped off, watching, catching a hint of the land of childhood in their veins, knowing that roots awoke impatiently with buds, sweet offspring driven by water. But inside the houses, where walls and partitions unfolded, inconvenient, full of crannies to hide love, meaning, and revenge, soft cushions that embraced the body, doorways that trembled in storms, stained-glass windows with rosettes and ribbons that colored light without destroying it, no one felt the wood or sand, and the absence of light or its waning was so different each day that it provoked arguments between the ladies of the house and maids; it was only the sign to light the lamps and say it is now too late for children to still play on the sidewalks of Scheller Street in front of doorways and windows and beneath the poor trees that had not lost the blackish coating of winter. Mothers called to nursemaids: that's enough, it's time for them to come in and wash, they've had enough fun, enough insisting and begging and promising, they've played enough games, bring them in, light the entryways, wash their noses and hands, change their shoes, comb their hair and give them clean kerchiefs; and the nursemaids obeyed.

In the moment of the almost violet light Miss Esther slowed her step, dressed in pure white without any color or jewelry or brooch or buckle or grace note to distract from the whiteness, returning to the house on Scheller Street thinking about the honest job of printer as the only treasure and even as a pretext to plan the impossible. But there was something more, something indistinct and nameless that shook when she cleaned out chests of drawers, rolled up the rug in her room in anticipation of summer, and bought a new piece of clothing and had to decide which old one it would replace; something that had happened in her home without a mother and with prayers, where her father dreamed and spoke both for pleasure and to tie her to that dream; something that she ought to recall and could not; something that at times seemed to have to do with austere, dark, almost bare rooms, with high ceilings and floors that creaked; something she had done or had tried to do. That was all: the memory became forgotten, forgotten since she was born, and like a strict taskmaster, it blocked her way. She could not force her way into the past, she could not look at it unless she wanted her flesh to become stone and salt, and no, not that. Memory had borders like countries, barriers, intricate passageways for which she did not know the password or she had lost it crossing one of these doorways and went astray, came to a stop in her own room in no way austere or cold or bare in the boardinghouse of Madame Helena Lundgren, everything blue, sky blue, snug and secure in winter, separated from the world up in the cold air, the colder the stronger to keep her from falling; windows open, the house, the street, the city, the world in summer a sounding box, echoing wall, mirroring water, singing landscape, golden frames for mysterious doors, decoy and disguise, and then she was helplessly weightless and no one fit where they belonged. Here the trail was lost, it was impossible to follow even the shadow of this suspicion about something that had perhaps never happened, which was not an event but an image on the polished surface of a door of a festive store and yet, yet; but now she did not know what she was trying to do with this venture and her shoeless white feet were taking her to the shadow, the moment, the insidious paw so silent as to be invisible, the night wrapping the bases of streetlights, night in the gutters and thresholds and in the jaws of gargoyles.

17. The Fabulous Animals of the Moon

Imagine an animal, ten, eleven animals, one hundred, too many, all the animals of all possible worlds, too many animals to count galloping across the plains of the moon: all the children in the houses on Scheller Street had heard about Count von Zeppelin and Co.'s dirigible, about trips around the world, but had not been able to learn anything more and essential, just what they wanted to hear, except by asking nursemaids or servants who could tell them nothing, since at dinner or practicing piano or during visits they could not ask and those who did not know it was forbidden got a freezing stare that promised punishment, the worst of all not being allowed to go out and play; little thoughts kept tight in pockets with the other children in the other houses on Scheller Street. All the children in the houses on Scheller Street imagined dirigibles as vast machines covered with sharp iron hair standing up like goosebumps, precise telescopes, toothed wheels, lances, and cords, jumping from star to star to take them to the moon where, like furious heroes, they would fight beings that came out of the night, as blurry and unthinkable as bodies that became restless only during fever; where, as triumphant spectators, they would watch parades of troops of lunary turtlets, schools of lunamatic shrewers, droves of lunacule buffalodonts, flocks of lunacious black vulturery, fighting with hoofs, horns, and claws, tongues covered with giant needles, leathery trunks and tails, killing and dying, winning and losing in simple and perfidious games like bouncing a little silver ball on the closed balconies of the houses on Scheller Street. All children, or perhaps not all, perhaps only the most bold or solitary or zealous or anxious had or sought a corner of the house somewhat like a cul-de-sac, like an eggshell where no one went, a noiseless corner where they could hide to try to put words together with balls of string, a hidden clearing in a jungle of curtsies, grown-up foolishness, contradictions, and shadows made with interlaced hands on a white wall, keys to enter the dark cave where all the tribe's secrets were guarded, all of them, not a single one lost or deteriorated with the years, and this, although it was not one of the games they dreamed about at night or played during the day, depended precisely on those games in a more direct way impossible.

Madame Helena took a black velvet skirt from the closet and hesitated a moment, telling herself that soon, if not already, velvet was not right for the season, and perhaps a cameo, too, but then even more rightly soft flannel instead of velvet, a blouse with a plain neckline that would accommodate a necklace and ring set, the green enamel one with the silver drop and chain. She knew she could never buy pearls like the ones that Madame Nashiru had brought from Montijo Bay or Kiushu, ship by ship, from the lips of meleagrina clams to exhibitors standing on parquet flooring or to smooth white silk trays, pink pearls that seemed hardly touched in the glass display cases where careful hands had placed them. It was easier to imagine a thousand, a hundred thousand animals than one animal; hair, feathers, claws, spots, stripes, horns, udders, and muzzles had no need to be in place when there were a hundred thousand million animals dashing in a race to the bottom of the craters of the moon. A cloud of silvery dust, as moondust must be, was enough with thunder, clattering hoofs, chomping mouths, and who could crush whom and who flee from whom in the icy desolation, ashy as frost. From the end of the street, from the ravines of the moon the victorious bray of turtlets arose like a hurricane and stole into Madame Helena's ears, who left the skirt on the back of a chair and forgot the pearls to her regret, diminutive pearls, perfect spheres of albescent irritation. Shouts that split the cold air like glass thorns, impertinent running around, the sheer stupidity of mothers and nursemaids who let little boys play in the street, and even, she had once seen and hardly believed, girls out so late. Meanwhile, behind Madame Helena's back and with some haste because the afternoon was getting dangerously late and at any moment front doors would open and formidable figures would order them to put an end to that and come inside immediately, the turtlets insisted on another race fleeing from colossal feet and waving trunks, and then they had an idea for salvation, and not from the other side of the moon: no more battles, instead they could play Trapsnare so their shouts would not be heard inside the houses. Some children were against it, cautious souls already well versed in prudence: there was little light and for Trapsnare someone would have to go in to get chalk and would not be let back outside so one of the teams would be a player short and they would also need seeds as counters, or buttons or little stones, and the cooks and servants would raise a fuss if they tried to get them. Madame Helena put away the velvet skirt and, on the marble-topped table, put the rings and the cameo with the clover-shaped cross and the profile of a woman whose hair was swept up and held in place with an ivory ribbon for a headdress with three malachite birds and golden threads. She did not like children; she was grateful to fate for not having them, although at times this thanks was not only vain but unjust; perhaps her body had refused, wisely closed, renegade and resistant to the threat that it could have inexplicably and proudly become swollen by the Linz doctor. It seemed to her that her life was not a bright ribbon like the one that united the three birds on the ivory-crowned woman whose cameo profile matched the rings, not a series of events arranged on another ribbon that was time; instead it was an attempt, a test in thin air, a resolve so consistent, so certain that only by being quiet and hushed, unconnected and unheroic, without anger or haste, could she manage to discern its opaque whole. In another way, she could never know her part of the anxiety, meanness, exaltation, or vague ambition of other people, never relate to the hidden letters in the odor of the Linz tobacco factories, the poems by Asa Lundgren that her mother recited, the trip north, the objects that she had kept in her parents' home and those she had gotten rid of, the walls she had marked to be removed to create another space, the ones she had erected to enclose another room, her selection of the guests for the house, the empty room, that strange girl, Madame Nashiru's pearls and Madame Nashiru herself, the mysterious selection of the enemy and of black as the denial of all color for her clothing although permitting herself the whim of a bit of green or autumn yellow, rigorous limits otherwise acceptable within the rights she deserved.

Sometimes, but not on this uncertain afternoon on Scheller Street, they played Take the Fort, War Between Nations, Prisoner's Base, and Jump the Fire. For the animals on the moon, an ability to detect allies on one hand, and speed, strength, and slyness on the other, meant triumph for those lunar animals, letting them swagger on the way to school the next day. Children? Tender innocent creatures? Incomplete men, miniature adults filled with laughter and adorable traits? There were games more secret and suffocating but not in the street, arms held behind backs, breath held from fear and shame, other hands lowering pants, or wet mouths declaring the tests they would have to pass to become men. Men? Such fear, seriousness, distrust, silence, hidden trembling, cold indifference, and control of eyes and hands? In Madame Helena's rooms there were two mirrors and she passed before the two each night after dressing as she walked toward the door. She entered the corridor, and as she neared the stairs, she looked out the window down at the street, now almost dark.

18. Only His Eyes

It must have been a charm, a charm that had hung from a chain on a woman's neck, or an earring, or almost certainly a talisman, a fish-man that conjured storms and attracted schools of fish to nets, in which case it would never have sparkled at a woman's neckline; on the contrary, women would be banned from even looking at it because women and the sea, women and ships, women and fishing were a bad pair that brought endless misfortune, poverty, rot in the soul, and death in life. Perhaps in that case it would demand a tithe, how could it not if it could be avid and cruel but not always, if it could change with the light, time of day, season, and possessor; Mr. Pallud had known all that immediately in the store when it was nothing more than a little pile of promising metal, formless and waiting for only his eyes and touch; on the other hand it could be agreeable and generous in the morning, he suspected, but to see that he would have to wait until the next day, an entire night's vigil with waterfowl, water to make dry land fertile, water currents that a ship left behind in its wake like his would, what fish breathe, and what its old silver, made from embers and scales, would reclaim. With his hand in his jacket pocket on the charm, he walked streets silent only for his ears, the light growing fainter, still not sure where he would put it. Would he know when he arrived, would he say here, would he feel the proper arrangement rising from his curved fingers up his wrist and arm to arrive in his brain? Or would doubt swirl like a whirlpool, truly waterlogged, mocked by uncertainty, not knowing what to do? It seemed to him, did it not, that true happiness was drowning him, that today he could, if he wished, sadly and quickly rid himself of all his treasures and keep only the fish-man no larger than one of his fingers, the ring finger, yet more gigantic than Cronus, able to fill all his shelves, cover the window, take over his rooms. He could enclose it, not really, he knew, but he could force his hand to close over it, and what was it his hand held, a shadowy tithe that he would pay possibly for his whole life or for just a few minutes; he could tie it up with string so nothing could escape, call Kati-Kati and tell her to throw it in the trash, without bothering to look at her as he spoke. Never had he had an unnameable presence so close: he often entered those vile little stores in which an old woman in rags warily croaked an impossible price for a bit of a shipwreck, and, although from time to time he would discover something worthwhile, he was accustomed to leaving those holes vexed and empty-handed. Inevitably mad, those old women pulled their dirty shawls tighter against the distant sea wind, loath to admit what they did and did not wish to sell, and this time behind that nasty woman from whom he had never bought anything, on the edge of a book that stuck out on a forgotten dust-covered heap, there was a little pile of metal that for him and only for him shone through long-gone water because otherwise how else could he have seen it? He stopped short, caught, staring, remembering that he would need to pay, not knowing if it would be for his whole life or just a few minutes, while he asked the old woman about the base of a lamp, the beads from a necklace in a broken cup, and the fish-man curled up on his cornice, murky from abandonment, dirt, and waiting. He almost stopped, no, he did not, he walked as if he were troubled, especially in the store compared to now in the street, fabricating indifference again on his face and gaze as if he did not want to haggle, as if the talisman did not interest him, but it did, he could not part from it, move his hand, open it and leave it somewhere and turn and talk about something else, but the old woman, farther from him and it than anything, had declared the three prices and left him to pay what he wanted without looking at him or it. Yet he knew he was in the street, he knew he was not far from the boarding house of Madame Helena, he knew that he was going to arrive and the fish-man was going to slide down the corridor, blazing, immortal, and unique, but in a mood that made men dream, he was still just outside the doorway of the nasty little store, now with his hand wrapped around the charm. In spite of impending nightfall, he could already hear the shouts of children playing on Scheller Street, they told him where he was and pulled him from his stupor. A charm? When he was in his rooms he would put it under a light to study it and see if the oval head did or did not have marks of broken or ripped metal that would tell him if it had ever hung from a chain, and if they were there he would file them off until they disappeared to make it into what it had always been. While he did not want to think about the setting, the reign, the water that would bubble up wherever he put it, or think about the treasures he would have to displace, set aside, move, or put away, the violinist, the bear, the shepherdess, the gargoyle, the mill girl, the sorcerer, the farm animals, the smith, the reader, the ballerina, the fat man, he did want to think about the blank notebook page in which he would mark it down as if it were one more item but with different handwriting or a different color ink, and he would note it as something he knew not yet what. As he took another step toward the house he recalled the hanged man who well past death would grimace if he blew on him to make him spin. How could he know or not know if the fish-man was not the executioner who carried out irrefutable sentences, a malign toy that he should have left with the leather-faced old woman in the cave of a store darkened by filth.

Heindesberg would not be much help because Heindesberg only considered what was possible; he thought for a moment, pausing near a wall because there were other people in the world and they were even walking down this street, about the possibility of going to the municipal library the way the General went to the museum library and looking, looking for what? A history of aquatic religions, an essay about anthropomorphic animals, men with dog heads, eagles with women's breasts, giants with lion haunches, serpents with girl's faces, sirens, vampires, toads that talk, tortoises with hands, birds with lips; a bestiary, the oldest one there was: a nightmare zoology. He would see them in the jungle world and not in books, he would recall them, whether for his whole life or just a few minutes he did not know, he dared to be sure of that, he would guess what they were as they climbed and hung head-down from the highest branches of the most colossal trees, swimming upstream in the iridescent rapids at land's end where ships disappeared toward other horizons. What toothy faces, what feet divided into a thousand joints, what ostentatious headdresses, what other life, what inscriptions on what walls would be his when the fish-man decreed another destiny and Scheller Street was less than a memory lost in the thick dust of nasty little second-hand stores. He believed he was at the point of discovering an order not very secret yet truly eloquent about how to turn the future into an inevitable landscape, a familiar scene which had always been there and for that same reason was only seen during visits or when the dice had fallen in one of those atrocious games commonly called games of chance, or fate, or god, and even then, with all the rest deprived of its transitory sense, the color of curtains or the arrangement of chairs around a table could be viewed without understanding them; but the instant passed without having shown him even a yellow fig dripping sweet juice, and he soon found himself almost at the house of Madame Helena, wavering in the half-light, his head echoing with the shouts of a hundred, thousand, million children who played on the canvas of the street, shouts like horns, like a trap, like a difficult to escape flood, where he did not know whether he had been turning things over in his mind for his whole life or just a few minutes.

19. Youth, the Reddened Warrior

So often compared to vineyards or deer, upon closer inspection youthful bodies better resemble something invisible and dangerous, streams of energy it is inadvisable to approach like edges, parapets, and fire, ready to burst or to cushion heavy falling objects, unfortunate people, withheld affection, or whatever is hidden in incompletely clear intentions or even dreams, nostalgic for the Golden Age; young Gangulf, for example, thin and fast yet with a confiscated rage that he tried to control and felt sorrowful if he failed, more than satisfied if he could save it for random moments in the darkness of a park, behind a carefully closed door, or in a church before the flaming eyes of the images of saints in torment. He was not studying, because the letters in his books lay there like ants, like distant tropical ants with potbellied lustrous queens leading armies, like the blackest fastest ants or white ones tunneling through wood with lighting-fast metallic mandibula gnashing in the light before his eyes, malignant things, nightmares on dry mornings, mirrors that deformed small-town afternoons with their half-open windows; they stretched madly and were useless, so useless he could slam the covers shut, throw them hastily on the table, yet bear in mind *Of the Power of Souls* because he had been defeated: more than senses exist to place man in contact with a world where he had been born defeated to a life that surrounded and crushed him, but, for all that they deny the existence of an invisible force and tell him if it exists, its presence is perhaps not necessary, he had always liked to believe in it; he had been born to lose and this exonerated him, and even if they denied this presence of a hidden force, it made him throw his books on the table one against the other, jump up, look for his hat gloves cape, gestures that were just that, gestures assaying excuses for certain acts perhaps rightly called mad if taken in their totality, empty orders that must be complied with the way empty soup tureens and secret compartments in rings for poison must be filled, inscribed in the hidden being that responds to omnipresent nature, the immanent vision arising preformed entirely from the Highest; with three books under his arm, his hat brim tipped over his eyes, gloved hands to hold the cape against his deerlike body, hiking against the boxed-in wind down the university street asking what might allow an imperfect creature to perceive another reality, that of the Spirit undoubtedly, taking too-slow obligatory steps in search of ants: the true moral color of actions, the unmentionable hue of decisions, the breadth of talents, the other perspective of sin, the savannas of Africa, the green plains of the Americas where brittle desert ants dine on the marrow of yellow-tufted animals spread and cooked on embers, and thus the blind have to see more than those whose eyes are sound there where they domesticate boas and race mounted on jaguars with necks longer than giraffes', mutes who make their voice heard to the ends of the earth, the deaf who hear the fall of a strand of cotton amid thunderous machines, and yet one dies slowly in nitrate mines devoured by the sun and worms emerging from beneath the white crust which has become one's skin and where monsters sit on tree trunks, angels in huts and fools in palaces, the highest and lowest of the arc created by the impulse of Power. So at night, returning on the route to the black open windows, remembering, careful and ready to escape if necessary: he knew what he would find in the eyes of Miss Esther if he could

look her in the face, make her look at him in the face and thanks
to that awaken, shed the obstinately worded text composed with
utmost patience, hurry and meet her again in the doorway. She
might flee, which comforted him. Perhaps Madame Helena did not
totally trust him despite the circumspect letters from his father, but
then, had not the silly Esther fallen in love with him, the sweet miss
in sweet blue and gray behind her sweet sugar counter? He would
not arrive in time and this would bother him the way everything
incomplete did at night, it would be awful like the savannas of Africa
next to the pulpit for the almighty five senses and as a result the
body was now dangerously empty, the walls worn out, the tapestry
of daydreams still unconfessed, and he launched himself ahead,
toward the deer park like an incendiary arrow burning everything it
passed, and the air came to a stop and made lustrous ants explode
between the teeth of the distant and ever-patient horses.

20. Fountains

He believed, shielded by years of waiting and fire, that there were beings fragile due to their intricacy, a tangle of little cells, honeycombs, labyrinths, knotted partitions, and beating vessels the width of a hair, hands so very tiny, impassive as white insects but soft, incapable of holding anything of wood or metal, incapable of holding themselves if they fell, holding on to something and staying there; fragile bodies, brittle, and indecisive, not fully finished, imperfect and vacillating like shrill music or the dying flame of a candle that no longer gives light; bodies that enclose a thread of awareness, a stirring of reason that calls to the storm and desire like obsession, like the need of some long-legged insects to pose blind on a despotic arm, their dead fragments blemished. Impossible to know or even suspect what was schemed behind those eyes where orders ought to rebound, echo, and be obeyed. He had seen these ill-endowed beings, like a defective hand of cards that should be returned, in the rows of faces that passed for review, eyes opaque and buttons shining, and knew that something had to be taken from them, knew that they were going to sob and break but in the end he was going to obtain what he wanted, the perfect men whom their fathers had dreamed of upon engendering them because who and where was the man who did not carry that dream and release it at that moment, the vision of purity and perfection, a single back for all to receive the designation like a lashing with a single look, a single leap for the hero. He had known how to manage them but not now, now it was impossible to reckon hidden solidity because the shudder at what had dawned now filled him with the ardor of the desert sun, the torrent, the cavalry he charged against full force to conquer those things that had been impossible in the splendor of campaigns. Not anymore, so he had abandoned any attempt and merely looked, blind before weakness, an attempt like a light that swung a delicate body back and forth. Nonetheless he had not been able to ponder pearls because only by chance he had never gotten near hellebores or wildflowers, and these links to something greater than chance were precisely what had to be eliminated for victory. But in fact, as strange as it might seem, he had learned to be in the presence of things he had never expected: fountains, for example. Outside of his room in the boarding house on Scheller Street, the only things that had interested him were cleanliness, the sheen of pottery, the polish of marble, untainted plates, the shine of bronze, barely visible glass, and waxed wood: he had not known nor had wanted to know anything else, but ever since Madame Nashiru arrived at the house, he had been given to imagining within the wall what until then had been mute, fountains of soft porous material, viscous even beneath fingertips, and the satin feeling that slides all along rounded moldings. He had sunk to the point of keeping his hands in his pockets to avoid bas-reliefs, the eyes of unknown flowers touched by someone who with almost all certainty was not him, and water splashing a naked body that he wanted to correct into soldierly excellence, not the admixture of a confused novice, instead ready for the cruelest test. He was able to recall that in those cases water, the most innocent thing in the world, could become a condemnation, like salt or wood, and all in silence so as not to lose what little the victim was allowed to keep. Only then was it certain that a man was not going to retreat; only then was he sure about the echo and could give himself orders.

Magnificent bodies that he supposed were gilt; black in death, it was true, but golden or ivory below rough clothing, gems and tight belts on the hips, slipping and colliding with each step or stride, not with dance, not with the footstep barely audible in the corridor when he was waiting, having returned to his room after breakfast. And in the street harder than sands or salt pans or mountainsides, at an indecent speed in the street, came the wonder of hidden feet that upon being placed bare in fountains would cloud the melting water: men submerged, motionless, gilt in freezing water, made of dangerous ivory, up to the belt without a moan, without a grimace, conquered like a trophy. The General did not like to shout, he would never gallop down the hills of the moon howling after stampeding herds. He lost the sight of the pale silhouette between the afternoon shadows, he strove to shorten his step like an offering, with the same unspeakable weight in his chest, cold sweat on his temples, and in the repertoire of never considered scenes, he finally imposed, as in his worst nights, the mastery with which he would use his hands, belts, and the innocence of water to create fragile strength. He heard screams because he would invoke screams, he had heard the injured scream and better yet the prisoners: screamed until they could scream no more, he would oversee it, screaming like the screams he now heard, yet as he turned the corner to Scheller Street, no, it was the children as they played who screamed when someone opened a door, when someone arrived, when a lamp was lit, when a coach came racing from the craters of the moon, orange-yellow sparks from the hoofs of the horses on the round, swollen cobblestones, like the marble rosettes of the fountains.

21. Opera

As she would never do on any stage whatsoever, where she always had to act severe and haughty regardless of the heroine she was singing that night and whether the tatters of the Fiordiligi wardrobe scattered on the floor frightened her, Madame Simeoni, sunk deep in her cushions, covered, hidden, and stentorian, moved her grand buttocks on the seat of her armchair. She had recently discovered how to change her position without too much effort and most of all without Nehala realizing she could do it: she pressed her hands and forearms against the armrests softly at first, then with increasing strength beneath the shawls and blankets, leaned just the littlest bit forward from the waist, dropped her neck and head between her shoulders, and who would have known how marvelously the muscles and tendons went up and down on the large pillow she sat on and relaxed, almost lost contact or as she liked to think all contact disappeared, and from that moment the only thing that remained for her to do was move the lower part of her body, the left half first, then the right, toward one side, toward the other, also forward or backward if she had spent too much time seated against the chair back. She sighed, which managed to make Nehala look at her, but now it did not matter, she could even think that this was what she had been seeking, to make Nehala look at her without needing to call her attention. Would they go down to the dining room tonight? No, they would not, there was not enough time now for Nehala to dress her and arrange her hair; she also remembered that they had gone down the previous night, and she knew it was best not to be too generous with herself, to be there all the time like the Chinese woman or the old idiot. It was preferable to be absent from time to time; she smiled thinking about what they would ask, what they would say, what they would suppose, while she was wrapped in a world of tulle, gauze, ribbons, and crowns: the sacrificial tunic, whatever was required for her to stand out, count the beats and raise her head, magnificent, as if she could make out their faces and hats, sip again the sweetness of the golden liquor, far from the applause. Floria Tosca was an idiot, obviously, although no more than Norma, and she had never wanted to sing Leonora because Azucena was too powerful. Aïda, that was her favorite. There had been so many things on stage, marbleized columns, capes thrown over a chair, stained-glass windows, screens, staircases, and more humble objects, writing pens, a lute, a mortar, dried flowers, a hammer, where had there been a hammer? a kerchief, Desdemona's, and when injured Nedda tried to escape, Silvio and Otello appeared and stabbed her, it was Otello, wasn't it? and Alfio killed Turiddu: the comedy had ended, which was a pity because Nehala was coming on stage. Madame Simeoni, head held as high as at the end of the second act, looked at Nehala as she drew close, Aïda, she thought, Amneris was very much a princess, but Aïda, that was her favorite, she could sing her again with just a few rehearsals, sing Aïda again as she had that time in Buenos Aires. She did not want Nehala to dress her, she did not want to go down to the dining room. The people there talked too much and it bothered her; when she sang conversations and even insignificant noises bothered and distracted her: they should be quiet. Nehala assured her that the voices did not come from the lower floor but from the street, where children ran around shouting, and Nehala seemed satisfied with that. She did not insist on dressing her and doing her hair to go down to the dining room, she walked right past her armchair to look out the window at the children playing in the street.

22. The Red Moon

Of the nineteen possible orbits of the moon that Aristarchus of Samos postulated and which according to him depended on the fifty-seven movements of the Earth around the sun, a theory that won him not mere suspicion but scorn from his contemporaries, there are three that can slide open the bolt on the door of madness in men's souls: the so-called elastreon (from ελαστρεω, move forward), the neopostic (from νεωποιεω, erect a temple), and sinomic (from σινομα, damage, injury, harm). It was later said that the coachman had suffered an attack of red madness due to the lunar trajectory that night; also that the gentleman for whom he was driving had jumped into the coachman's seat, snatched the whip, and had lashed the horses with an untiring arm; and finally, that the shouts of the children as they played in the street had frightened the animals. Some authors maintain that Aristarchus of Samos had a happy childhood, which one may suppose took place beneath blue skies on white beaches where he would picnic and play with azure stones before submerging his feet and eyes in the sea, something that almost certainly cannot be said about the other Aristarchuses who wander through history with their exiles, always-frustrated ambitions, envies, dire illnesses, and terrible deaths. But the Aristarchus who designed the nineteen possible orbits of the moon and thought of death as more of a transit, an innate coloration that obscures the perseverance of life as it grows and spreads, would have comprehended in an instant the inclination toward misfortune that night on Scheller Street when there was no more light in the sky, and comprehended the way Katja understood it when she shouted without knowing how the shout had arisen in her throat, and thanks to Luduv she had always known how to fill the silence that no one but her perceived.

Only the lights revealed by the windows and balconies, only the sparks from the horses' hoofs, only Samos's unsteady moon that did not yet face directly into the street, still rising behind respectable buildings after having dragged itself through the alleys and taverns next to the river, only that light and the soul's red madness which is less garish, less than a dashing torch, less than a votive flame: there was only that light and no more, so it was logical that Madame Nashiru did not know what to say after it was all over, shielding herself in her condition as a foreigner so she would not be called to testify by a knock on her door, perhaps even looking for her behind the curtains in the back office without windows in the "Pearls of the Orient" jewelry story to urge her to remember with elusive precision the confused moment in which she prepared to cross the street, attentive only to the step she was about to take from the curb to the pavement. It would be unfair to say that Madame Nashiru as a girl had not played on white beaches beneath porcelain skies because not only had she done so but she had also had little soft feathered animals and picture boards, abacuses, rattles, tiny mother-of-pearl trees, and miniature carts. When she heard the thump she was not thinking about lost childhood or certain death in the thunder of racing animals; she was not thinking about pearls, about the strange world of the sea or tortoiseshell combs, wide silk sashes, bright threads, or the separate partitions of a house trembling during storms. To tell the truth, she was not thinking about anything: she looked up at the far end of the street and saw beyond the runaway horses, beyond the coach and trees and silhouettes of houses darker than the dark night, beyond Aristarchus of Samos although she did not know it was him waving the paper lantern that she thought was the moon, to the time when she was too small to arrange pieces on a playing board and too big to stain the white silk of her dress with fruit preserves. Someone had told her once that eyes of wonder see genies at crossroads, but for them, cardinal points are not the end of roads but yesterday and tomorrow, down and up, neither present nor here. It seemed to her that there was more light than before and that some absent hands were moving pieces on the playing board and that she would have to be alert instead of paying so much attention to sparks and the nineteen probable orbits of the moon. So she backed up over the curb again, one hand quickly raised to her cheek, the other clutching her purse so she would not drop it; while another hand deep in the pocket of his black jacket tried not to brush the metal of his keys against the fish-man, which rang, he did not know how but it rang, capered impatiently, finally liberated and free, freer than the first light of the sun, freer than the noise of the wind, and much, much freer than its owner. Mr. Pallud did not know how perhaps because it was not him but the fish-man who had made him fail to find the keys, let his hand rest quietly with his fingers barely curved between the stringy fabric of his pocket, then suddenly turn his head and see the carnival that sparks outlined on the dark ground. He had never disguised himself, not even with a mask, not even a small one as a prank or joke, or had hidden to jump out with a shout to frighten someone, or done anything that would make him transfer his soul disposed to red madness to another being for a moment, even just a second, to say nothing about white beaches but, yes, about the austere bedroom in which shoes poking out from the doors of the closet seemed to herald the lord of autumn's automaton made of dead leaves who wore those shoes, a courteous companion with agendas and obligations and an unknown master who did not show its power, immense as it was, waiting, and its power was in waiting. He was afraid then and about to close his eyes but he did not. He saw the coach pass: he let himself do that and not just that, he also clung to the fish-man, felt it grow inside his hand, smelled the metal made of molecules of his blood, saw with his own eyes death in the middle of the street, sated, a squalid smiling pig, fishy black, slow to disappear, heavy as indigestion from gold, gold from mountains, gold from rapid rivers, gold in veins in ritual caves; the same gold that shines in the teeth of the man that Lola finds prowling around her, surrounding her again and again as if she were calm but she is not, and he looks at her smiling, at times showing his gold teeth as if purposely, an upper front one very visible, the other one only when he opens his mouth and she sees it shine by the light of the candle at the head of the bed in the back of his jaw like a warning. But Miss Esther alone and in white without anything golden or any color to relieve it did not see the sparks from the horses' hoofs on the stones or the fireworks that had frightened them: she hid her face against her father's shoulder who softly laughed at her fear and said but my child, what are you doing, for she would cover her ears when she saw the malignant flash of lightning through the curtains, hold her ears tight and close her eyes so firmly the lids wrinkled, never hearing the thunder that choked and drowned her although it lasted on and on only for a few seconds. She only saw the back of the coach and heard the gallop and noise of wheels on stones, only saw something in the middle of the road, a lighter-colored shadow, a mere nothing, something that frightened her more than thunder, something silent and not bellowing, but something that shook her from her torpor and demanded her attention like childhood maps, like Mr. Celsus's jokes about colors, like a portrait artist's work, like women's eyes. There were maps on the walls of her childhood bedroom, maps ripped from an atlas her father had bought in Wielischplatz that continued to hold up the colossal cloudy

Heavens even without its covers, index, and references: maps of Iceland, Livonia, Martinique, Hajis, Mahé, Tubuai, Yannson, Peru, Jabal-Shammar, Ceylon, and Swaziland. There was a town in Brazil called Aguapeny and a port in Ecuador called Zorritos and a river in Columbia called Mururuti and a place in Argentina called Llao-Llao. All of this and time made up the world, all this and a single instant is the sum left to the heir, dressed in white seeing without knowing in what instant it would come. She had played with letters, too, but this had to be before the maps, painted on colored cubes, and she threaded little stones with holes drilled into them and she took them off the threads, pushing them with her fingers that moved quickly, squeezing and squeezing until her skin burned on the little cord so she could hear them like a rattle of hailstones on the table and floorboards: looking for the beads that fell was part of the game, to call them, to hear how they called to each other as they rolled on the floor, and to feel sorry for the ones that were lost and would never find their companions again; sad like Wulda scrubbing pots to hear Katja's shout and think that she was going to grow old and die scrubbing pots and would never get to rest like her mother in a bed next to the window waiting for the sun. The sun or perhaps the moon appeared on the horizon in the window of the kitchen and Wulda dreamed while awake for the first time, thanks to one of the possible orbits that Aristarchus of Samos had drawn, about salons of marble and glass, harp music, diamonds in her ears and a heavy dress with golden thread that covered her to her feet when she descended an imperial staircase. United to an uncomfortable and free Lola and to Katja who saw what no one else did, united the way the world's trees were by their seven thousand times seven million roots, she felt herself separate into fragments, more and more fragments of herself that were still her, scrubbing pots, and each fragment heard different music, words, sudden thumps, and shouts because she still had the ears of all the herselves in the kitchens and on the imperial stairways, discovering passages in the earth and innumerable orbits of the lights in the Heavens.

Upstairs Madame Helena and Nehala on far ends of the building heard the crash and if the afternoon had been kept distant from them by rain darkening the windows, they managed to see a tangle of hoofs, wheels, helmets, muzzles raised to the air like buffalodonts on the moon, arms in the air, legs foreshortened, and a useless whip that rolled over the paving stones. Madame Sophie Simeoni asked what had happened down there when she saw Nehala turn toward her pale, her mouth covered by both hands, one over the other, her eyes so wide that they were white all around, two frightened little staring black balls, but the truth was that Madame Sophie did not care and had asked just because, because the girl had turned so brusquely that she had to say something so that she would not give her another one of those frights again and at that moment could not think of any way to reproach her, but she did care about the cushions, shoes, coral necklace, and blanket already too heavy for the season. Nehala did not answer: her games had been played in the best reigns, in theaters, train cars, ship cabins, and she had played at being characters from operas: gypsy, tyrant, slave, Spaniard, poet, captain of the guard, but she never worried about the stories, she only played at what they were doing, sitting or still or dead or stopped in a dance step. She had possessed, and remembered it very clearly, an adored toy hidden so her mother would not pick it up, look at it, and ask where she had gotten it, a metal rose that the Countess Ceprano had used in the first act, kept it for years until it got tarnished and broken and she threw it into the sea during a voyage, perhaps the last one, a leaden-gray sea on a freezing winter afternoon when Aristarchus of Samos patrolled the frozen fire of the final stars. On the other hand, Madame Helena had played with hoops, jump ropes, swings in gardens, and blonde dolls who sat on diminutive hammock seats in playrooms: she chanced to see a body thrown forward, spinning, injured, beaten by the horses' hoofs, and she did not put her hands on her mouth but she did open her eyes wide without a shout or moan, leaning on the windowsill because she felt too heavy for her legs that she found were weak and shaking, and the coach went on amid shouts, after an instant or not even an instant of silence, held breaths, something that cloistered voices, suspended gesturing hands, and nailed feet to the ground. The General's boots struck the pavement in a victorious parade of war cars down avenues, bloody flags on the flagstaffs, minuscule bare feet stepping on glass beads in the basins of fountains, soldierly merits, naked bodies destroyed by blasts in the water that springs up like the gold of the earth. He thought, when he became aware of his surroundings, the body was hers and the pain of the votive became fury that sought an exit, emerged from concealment, tried to run, blood coagulating in his throat, knuckles white, the soles of his boots stuck to the soles of his feet and his feet like stone roots, dead, poor imitations, as he looked not at what remained lying on the ground after the coach had passed but at the gray motionless silhouette at the edge of the pavement, upright, light as the sound of clappers wrapped in felt that strike the bells in the houses of the dead, like the steps of predators in dense jungles, fragile, incomplete, trying to convince himself that she was calling him.

Young Gangulf might have wanted to shout but he could not and anyway it was now too late, everything had already happened as always, and as always nothing more remained for him but the final kingdom of the accursed hunger for gold, having finished only a portion of what he had proposed and not all of it, not always the easiest or the most pleasant, hanging like a little frog from the reeds in a marsh waiting for a downpour, for the distant intemperance, for the abysm he stared into every time he dreamed about what he would do and of the insipid pleasure in achieving it. His parents had given him complicated pivoting leather toys, self-propelled trains, ships that rode the waves in ponds, and armies of lead soldiers in fancy dress; they had provided playmates for his games, ordering the servants' children to always let him win, and had gone off traveling again. He wanted to master something and above all someone but not lowering himself on cords or turning on pivots but entering through the lips of open wounds, someone who would fear him and beg, although it was a forgettable stranger like that dead body that had started rotting from the instant it had begun to fall beneath the beast's hoofs. He happened to see Miss Esther but not on that night or ever could he force her to look him in the eyes because she knew a secret he did not, and he ran toward the useless, weak, warm body, a tiny thought like a lightless dart flying from the tips of open fingers toward the sky, just a lighter stain in the night on Scheller Street.

Part Three: Prodigies

23. Sunrise

Not even during the well-built and well-protected tea-time, no, thought Madame Helena, there is no silence like that in a house in the hours preceding dawn, and it does not matter at all to be sleeping with the windows open to the noise of the stifling nights at the end of summer, it does not matter if the street and sky enter bedrooms and drag themselves all the way to the foot of the bed, it does not matter how exposed the indoors are to the weather and wind outdoors nor how exposed overwarm bodies are to sudden cold, to the whistles and sirens that blow, to the murmur of the barges and tugboats in the river. In sleep, the world becomes the background of a shop window or simply disappears, crumbling like the painted friezes in old houses where humidity works surreptitiously from inside the walls; sleeping and caring about no one else after the last second of wakefulness and nothing is yet like it is going to be; the heavy bellies of houses puff up, sustain dreams and above all tears, like a dike and refuge, as if the houses do not know the people they protect, as if they had just welcomed them and were still not clear on their names, which one goes with which face, which bodies wear which clothes; they cope with fears, moments and days not yet amassed, tuille curtains piled up on a chair ready to be hung to block sun and light, thick syrups poured down the throats of women in labor, whispered calls, and serene mirrors perhaps comparable to frozen lakes in which the caves beneath the water's surface remain uninhabited and mute. In dreams, erratic sprits of lost Christmases dance in the windows, impossible colors shimmer in eyes, and whatever happens, it remains within the refuge of pillows: some people hear voices and some overcome their shyness, become their own rivals, form part of the landscape in a book of hours, or work in unforseen professions. Shining dragons; stone mortars where tired bones are milled, long tired leg bones, small flat bones of tired fat hands; deceptive silhouettes from a painful summer in which too many changes have had to be managed in the house; shadowy dragons obliging careful movements down corridors and stairs bearing in mind the time of day and everything that had been said on previous nights around a poorly served table. This during sleep, and by day meddling between the beginning and end of sleep when interruptions have been so bothersome they leave a scuff mark on doors, when mornings have been broken up by commotion and injustice, when there is too much to understand and concerted effort does not suffice for what has not yet taken form but has begun, but for the moment there are only suspicions, marks on the sand, and above all hopes that nothing will happen.

Then, it could be believed since the night and the house are still dark and it is time to sleep, at some moment for no reason, because a reproach has worn away the weft of a world that is trying to repair itself and behave as usual against the tide of what is happening outside, a silence arises and obliges knowing, organizing, not being fooled, running from store to store to learn the prices for everything sold and everything bought, with people present who have always known how to confront the changing series of waves about what is said, people who have not retreated or hidden behind faces devised for specific attractive lies. It is no excuse that the tranquility may not be of this world: the house has been there for a century, more than a century on Scheller Street, following the curve of the river, with its trees and gray facades and flesh inside, thoughts like the buzzing wing of an insect and desires turned into candies and colorful stitches resonating on the still-tense fabric stretched between framework, and the feeling of stagnant water, everything that happens and still has not and stops existing when it has: these thoughts need the grandeur of decisions. At that moment in which the still-missing light seemed to be about to peek over the curve of the river and rise up, erasing the shadow in the garden, Madame Helena Lundgren decided not to wait, not to accommodate, not to pretend anymore. Katja might or might not get well, no one could know, and although Wulda would remain, that was not the problem, she could not continue to serve dinner clumsily with giggles and excuses. She would look, discuss, compare, and at least attempt that very afternoon to have a new maid in the house, someone who knew how to serve food, present platters, fill glasses, and wait next to the sideboard, eyes always vigilant to see what every diner might need. She would need to prepare the suite on the ground floor that opened onto the garden that morning, not wait until the afternoon, and perhaps let Mr. Ruprecht come to occupy it. Somewhere a door softly closed and if she had been sleeping the noise would not have awoken her, but since she was yet in bed at the soft, best threshold of the day, a closing door could still change her mind about those very proper, almost perfect plans birthed by the house if she changed at that moment; a door that closed at that changeable moment could even make her think about the house in Linz which she never thought about or about Madame Nashiru's stone garden that she would never see, where women's shadows slide toward other shadows, threatening and triumphant, happy to destroy them. She sat up in bed and, as she did, she broke apart the fragile shell that sometimes holds memory at bay: memory, Madame Helena thought, should not be impeded; without wrappings, smoke, or jewels, it can easily be incorporated

ANGÉLICA GORODISCHER

into everyday life, the black and green border, the white porcelain that chimed in the dining room, open windows and balconies, steps in the corridor, Lola's creeper now almost reaching the grille on the first floor balcony, the doctor's visit—had Wulda spent another night watching over sick Katja?—the locksmith who would have to come to change the window catches in the kitchen, the tea she would drink in the dining room once all the guests had drunk theirs because Wulda could not go upstairs with two trays at almost the same time since Miss Simeoni no longer came downstairs for any meal, and she would ask for a coach to take Miss Esther and her luggage, which was not much, to the station at seven on the dot in the afternoon, and after that she could rest until the evening meal. She hoped that Madame Wunze would arrive when she said she would and not sooner to give her time to make the required renovations. She got out of bed and went to one of the windows: the summer did not seem to have ended, a scarlet line was sharply drawn, a sign from the gods about the day that had not come into being but would, over the river far from Scheller Street.

24. Luduv

And in a poor imitation of girls' sleep
in winter when morning lies in wait and sleep holds on so the
moment will not pass and doors open that were never there, Katja
in her room, smaller than Lola's due to hierarchy, where there are
two beds because for a time Madame Helena thought to have two
maids that slept in the house until the woman with the hats came
to offer her niece and Madame fired Louise and took Wulda who
worked harder and was stronger and quieter; this room that held
the sweat of nightmares but not the rhythm of hours spent sewing
or the labored silences of secrets, rocked a psalmody like a baby
in a cradle for itself and no one else, apparently mute and secret;
tasting all the letters of misery together while sighing, eyes closed,
such a placid face, the chest of winged beings shaking inside her
only for the mouth's remembrance of the flavor of nuts on sultry
afternoons, her body so unexpectedly flat beneath the blankets and
everyone believed that tomorrow, yes, tomorrow she would wake
as always and then, what a comfort, they could say it had been
nothing, a scare, hitting her head like that when she fell, poor
thing, a little sleep and convalescence but look at how well our
Katja is again, how easily she comes down the stairs and how she
smiles; meanwhile in the smoky whirlpool in her head, enclaves,
profiles on lost coins, angular time standing still, alleyways, and
the laughter when she began to be stuffed with images, dragged her

inside herself, fishing for pearls in Saboga, and was finally running after Luduv to find him under the eaves and in the embrace of the household to look out for him, to move in space and time through everything: people, for example, clocks, little stories, wooden furniture, foam, pages, glass and ink, groaning illness, sad freedom, hands that work in the quarry, and the rain that improves your hair; how lovely your blond hair is hanging over your forehead, Luduv, how lovely your eyes, Luduv, these gray wheels with a thousand stripes and the little black points that devour me, where I reappear at the blink of an eye and I am someone else because who is not changed by your gaze, seed pearls in the line of your teeth that I see when I hear you although you have never said it so precisely when May arrived on the breath of the ram and two threads of honey, for I was filled to overflowing with iridescence and do not want the world that turns, and I see you, I see us leave everyone behind; when you left, when I was not there, when I could not clutch the tails of your shirt, shake you by the shoulders to wake you and make you stay, trip you, make you stumble and fall with our legs intertwined and ours is mine again, to see you turn when I called you, Luduv! I called you because I could not be there or anywhere else if you were not there, and to speak of you to others to tell them that it had been a privilege but also to frighten you away, and since I could not find you among others I called you, Luduv! and there you were so serious, waiting to see what I would say, what I would do, how I would look at you and how I would welcome you and then you would know the reason why I caught up with you, this time it was no game, just to show I meant it, and I did not even know that it lay within me like the meeting of two rivers, a friendly pond filled with warm water to wash injuries; but seeing me, seeing me gloomy with white fists, raised and exposed without protection in the gray plain, or beneath sunny racks of vines and withstanding it all, you knew then it was not so, what your sister had filled with words, she who saw us both, who tolerated the wind and proclamations, orders, who had such a weak hold on life, held by spider silk, the devil's spit, the stigmata of a sliver, she was the one of the two who came down to this country, not sensitive to the cold there, deceptive and soft like betrayal, yet she was there and calling because she had lost everything when she lost you and I wept to see you and was left with nothing, the winged beings that used to come because you gave me back the threshing floor, the yoke, the warm manure on the black soil, they returned you and you gave me the echo of everything that has been said and sung and branches of coral, strings of pearls, strings of fish eggs, lianas, in a single presence the delirium of speech that has color and weight, the lime finally encrusted on the dinnerware, on the wall, in the clay baked in the back of the oven and tomorrow will be an eye as I will be the blue and gold world, I who delves, who announces, who lies, arc and oil lamp, and listen, she who sees you in the children's corner although there are no children, in the hoofs of the horses enraptured by fire on the stones, the polished marble that will be the gravestone or cheek or rim for water greener than the green young branch, where the ghosts cannot see, she who finds you in the embers and in the obstinate frost on the shortest day of the year, Luduv, shadow of my eyelids, cup for my thirst, stanza sung by basil on the windowsill, Luduv the lamb, harmony of my lips in prayer, the rocking of my hands, island of my eyes, sparkle of my mirrors, watchtower, water changing direction, color of my blood, pebble in my mouth, Luduv luminous mark of day, the name of music, beat, sparkling crystal, mysterious word in books, first hint of light, brother better known and loved for me than I myself, rock and spring, now, never, and always, the whole world and time, the whole sky, the bees, the sickle, riverbed, ivory and gems that only existed so we could be together through the veins in geography, because I am eye and you have been word, smoke, and wind, hidden life, the bones of the thick earth when the floods recede and shoots begin to rise up, because my hair ties you and the roots of all the world's trees rock us the way we rocked in our mother's belly and we will return again and again, Luduv, to reflect the eyes of plants, sail into waterways to live in Casabermeja or Naumi-Velé, bury betrayal, singing, Luduv, as we run from the voices of deserted throats, break glasses, raise up sandstorms, frighten and batter death, Luduv, and name ourselves.

25. Battles

The smell of coffee caught him looking at his feet: it was eight twenty-four in the morning and he was barefoot, dressed but barefoot, ready to go have breakfast after his long walk, wondering rather vaguely and indirectly, due to an imprecision that was plaguing him, about the possible need for another itinerary to seek the assurance that he had lost something insignificant at some point, a little thing that had interrupted the rhythmic mechanical movement that was his life. It was insignificant, barely a wedge, axis, or valve, something wholly unsuspected due to its size, as banal as the last toe on that left foot, and yet it had held him captive in front of the biggest fountain in Krieger Park waiting for the sun to rise or sitting on the bed breathing in the smell of coffee and looking at his bare feet. As always, he still trusted the darkness; he believed that there in the shadow, without moving, he could better overcome a sudden attempt by blood to leave his body, who knew if it was because shadows were dark like blood in battles, like platoons of dead men scattered on a hill or sunk into a delta that no one had to worry about anymore. He felt he must continue to contain not only his blood but all liquids within his unfaithful body, not let them escape, not permit them, once spilled, to reunite in the growing outer darkness, to protect himself and help his body withstand lengthy hours and days. And yet, if he were to cross the corridor diagonally toward the side of the house that faced the garden, he would leave the darkness and find the light from the glass door and nothing more: nothing more and it would be the wrong move, like having amassed an impulse that would never be resolved with action. He would review battles in the library at the first desk to the right, he would reconsider them from the point of view of the winners and the losers, and correct positions and plans. He would compile this into a book, the battles of the world by General Rainer von Gerthmann, which would show how it would have been possible to win the ones that had been lost, and to win those that had been won better, faster, and with fewer casualties; he would do it, put on his shoes, go have breakfast, and then be ready to begin the exposition of the first battle: first he would make a detailed description of his own tough, strong body entering the little grove of birch trees by the east flank, blindly determined and with no need to give it excessive attention but accidents in the terrain will no doubt require an earlier exploration with hands, fingers, their soft fragile gloveless tips touching each stone, each fountain, each lobe, each eyelash, and above all the navel, where, they say, orientals drive in their curved sabers to disembowel their despicable bodies and fall laboriously forward to die on a cushion of blood and viscera. To lie down on a cushion of blood like the dead who might not have died in battle: it takes five men to move, aim, and fire a cannon and they must not be killed, five well-fed, well-clothed, healthy men free of desire or resentment, each one's eyes on his assigned mechanism and nothing else; tough, impassioned men ready for the endless toil of war machines, of armored vehicles, the plumed hat for saluting the multitudes, men like him given to cut through the fabric of dreams and guard each hour so that not a minute would be lost beside the fountains in Krieger Park in the deepest dark of the dawn of day. Without a doubt leaving Mr. Kämpfer behind with his eyeglasses and smile and always-clean pens ready to make notes in blank books at the library, entire populations evacuated and Mr. Kämpfer with them, so he could reconnoiter the terrain like someone on the lookout for victory, but that could wait because once the enemy was decimated, its leaders captured, lesser prisoners exchanged for some man who had fallen into their hands because that was also inevitable, a few tortured as a lesson, flags flying, new maps drawn, the results of lightning conquest or disaster reported, he could leave and eat the breakfast that was getting cold on the table and, barely warm, it would reach his lips, tightly closed so blood would not try to escape, bubbling up in the pure night and overcome by the strength of old discipline. Once the enemy was dead, there would be no pity compassion mercy pardon or sympathy, dead weaklings and fools and barbarians and those who wear pearls and offer greetings with gloved hands and bend at the waist in a bow to fall dead with the curved saber slashed through a neck, tearing through flesh fine as paper, and eyes that he would have wanted so many times to see open in just the instant when he jumped from shadow to shadow, like the one in battle who is always the first to snatch the flag of mortification. Dead and nothing remains of them, not even memories or hints upon waking when the inescapable actions of every morning are undertaken, and for the first time the key ring is not where it ought to be, where it has always been every morning, even the gloomy ones going back years and years, he would never know how many nor did he want to try to calculate them because it was impossible to count the years: cadavers could be counted in fields tainted by fires, by red moons, by whirlwinds of smoke, and by boasts that would seed future wars, but not the years that were lost, confused by the haste of minutes and the predicaments of hope, years that began long and clear and passed in a single speech with knells and young wine, ingenious convictions, pillage, and arrogance, to end waving arms and stamping feet in the depth of nightmares, magnificence under a park pavilion, the drone of water given shape by a basin, the inexplicable intruding woman rising up in the fog of breath.

A book that would enumerate weapons and make an inventory of the virtues of soldiery, that would have a section dedicated to the undesirable aspects of the enemy, where surly looks and transparent silhouettes could be erased, which would forever annihilate jumbled words and synoptic charts and maps and ink sketches and above all prohibit the most bloody hours of the night and also the time, five after eight, to enter the dining room in the morning after the hike to Krieger Park and back. A book that would clearly state the ways to fight, the ways to take eyeglasses out of the interior pocket of a jacket, the ways to die, to erect fountains that collect water from geysers, to forget for no reason, to describe apt bodies for victory fluttering down alert from eagle nests, to put on shoes, stand up straight, kill oneself, enter the dining room again, the library, the vestibule as if nothing had happened nor as if ice were rising in crags there, prepared to accept the wounded body covered by scabs, etched by scars, opened and finally stitched up so it might serve in another winning battle from the shelter of the door that leads to the dining room at five after eight in the morning in the house on Scheller Street.

26. Nehala

From her armchair, she could not see the fire in the fireplace, only the glow of the fire on the rug and the windows through which early morning light entered. The bed was unmade because that girl, not the one who fell down the stairs but the other one who seemed even more stupid, had come in to revive the fire but left right away on the pretext of breakfast downstairs, saying that no other room still had a fire going; she thought about how to answer but could not because the girl left right away over that breakfast thing in the dining room, obviously too fast after her insolence about the fire. It should not matter to a maid and if it did, she should not say so. Since she had not gone down to eat breakfast for a long time, she would go down that morning, she had thought about it the night before when she went to bed and she had even dreamed about it, eating breakfast in the theater beneath a grand chandelier of a hundred lights, Mimi or Gilda singing or someone, anyone else singing Norma or Desdemona, what did she care as long as she could eat breakfast on stage or in the dining room downstairs surrounded by people she could tell about her trips because she would travel, of course she would, what else was she going to do now but travel, not spend her whole life sitting in that armchair or lying in that bed in that room, no, she would travel, have breakfast on ships and trains, buy black idols in the heart of Africa, go to the Americas and marry a rancher and live on the savannas next to grand rivers, to look through other windows instead of those, windows that opened onto estuaries, saltpeter mines, jungles, oases, windows where the night would fall slowly and not like these where it came suddenly and worse hid her from the street rather than showing her as if she were on stage; and in any case she could eat breakfast or perhaps lunch or afternoon tea, not on a tray the way she did when she had to do as she was told and go see if that stupid girl was coming up with the tea or if she had forgotten what she had been asked to do. Madame Nehala Simeoni, alone, a frightened lady next to the fire, hidden, defenseless, her lips shut like a meleagrina martensis clam and her eyes like a mollusc's in the coldest seas of the world, sitting facing the windows, door to the right, fire to the left, and behind her the tiny room that had been her bedroom for so long, had a moment of hesitation, teetered on the very edge of the word she had resolved to never say, and fought bravely not to fall. She could because she had seen many things: tightrope walkers and jugglers incapable of error, trapeze artists and acrobats who leaped from one swinging bar to another in the air without a net, lifeline, or God; she had seen the eyes and dresses and fingers full of pearls of that woman who came from so far away and whom her mother had despised too much to even say hello; but she would not, she refused, fought not to remember, not to know, not to look back, not to say it; then she thought about that smiling woman who would not go where she would because she was so different and instead would travel from one sea to another and yet another like the birds that cry out because they emigrate alone, like the slaves in chains who kidnap the lady of the plantation and flee with her to the mountains when the curtain falls at the end of the second act. Outside the morning grew later and if it was true that she could no longer go down for breakfast in the dining room and that the more stupid of the two girls would bring it to her on a tray but without her having to go to the door to open it and see if she was coming since no one had ordered her to do that, yet it was also true that she could go down for breakfast, it would not matter if she were late, if she had not dressed earlier, in black as she ought to and not in the gaudy woolens that she could wear when she was alone in her bedroom when no one was going to see her, and if she went down when Madame Helena and her guests were already seated, the men would have to stand up when she entered and the women would turn their heads to look at her and they would all have to smile at her and talk to her, say something to her, the first thing that occurred to them, and she could answer them or not, and raise a kerchief to her eyes where tears were about to slip out from the lids, which was not true but she could fake it. She would talk about her trips because now, yes, she could travel, not spend all day sitting on that armchair: no, she would go, she would go to Berlin and Paris and then to the Americas, to Africa first to buy black idols and visit the ruins as well as the dens of the pearls which that woman had counted, to see how naked young men attacked and scattered them and rose up to the surface, and she could watch because they were like little animals that had no shame, almost boys without hair or beards and their hands full of pearls. She would go to the dining room that very day, without thinking about it, without turning it over and over in her mind again and again like someone playing with a earring or paperweight, something round and smooth in their hands sliding from palm to palm, slipping between fingers, almost letting it fall but no, holding it, squeezing it, caressing it, and passing it from one side to another, warmed, almost softened by repeated touch, yes, without further ado, she would go downstairs, if not for breakfast at least for afternoon tea, and she would take her tea with cream and sugar, not thick cream, she would mix in milk so it would not fall into the cup in huge drops, cream and a lot of sugar, and she would eat butter rolls or gingerbread or malt cakes and would quietly tell, as if she were talking to no one in particular, how she was planning a trip, a long trip that would take her to stages all over the world, to cabins on ships, compartments in trains, to Africa, to Japan first of all, then to Berlin and Paris, and to the Americas. She would hesitate no more, no, she would rock on creaking wicker armchairs next to the splashing salty sea, the voice, the door, the intrusion, the reflection of the fire on the rug, the threatening suns on the window, the lengthening morning, and the crunch of toasted rolls between her fingers and halting words; and at that moment when Wulda entered to make the bed, she abandoned it all, the trip, the sea, the rocking chair, now devoid of all intent, all the immensity shrunk down to one unspeakable word: gone. She was gone and never ever would be there again in the exterior suite on the second floor of the house on Scheller Street.

27. In This World

Dangerous times could befall the boarding house on Scheller Street if danger meant more than one warning, a kind of outbreak, a seemingly inevitable lack of control that led to disobedience because there were so many things to do, too many getting in the way of the most careful plans from earlier days, an impression or a mark that wedged its way perfectly into those empty moments of confusion or lack of energy, for either one could be the cause as well as the effect; the same people were not always involved because young Gangulf or the General or Miss Esther when she had "Miraflora" were hard to find in the house, since it often happened halfway through the morning when the most urgent tasks had been finished and it was time to begin to prepare everything for midday, which seemed so distant and in the next second so close. Curiously, Wulda was one of those who felt time slip past most sharply, but she could not in any way name that instantaneous wisdom: she knew something was happening and the day held danger, she knew that a very secret eagerness had been cast aside and nervousness had taken its place because she did not know if she could properly do a task that would have been Katja's if she were not ill; she caught her breath and a light exploded with a bang between her forehead and ears. In that moment she thought about Aunt Bauma's advice and looked at Lola but neither of the two could offer her help; Aunt Bauma because she was not there but at home shaking out paper and wet rags, squeezing out wet fiber, drying it on a grille over an alcohol lamp, driving those enormous needles into the grayish ball, wet but not viscous, which told her what was the exact moment when it was not too wet or too dry to start to give it the right form, skillfully, swiftly, such fast invisible hands, eyes watching as fingers gallop, stretching it suspended in the air toward one edge, then the other edge, then the other again, until the wet ball became a translucid disk and Aunt Bauma could slow the speed of her hands, not enough to rest but enough to sigh and moisten that which instead of dregs of paper and worn out rags was now tissue, a veil, a fragile and glowing gauze in the lacquer so thick it seemed solid in the tank, to take it out and begin again with rapid fingers and untiring eyes until soon on the table lay the perfect mold for the perfect hat for an elegant woman, a blonde or a wretch, young or foolish, who would wear it to stores and visits at four o'clock in the afternoon; and because Lola wandered around as if she were not there although she was, and had to remind herself to laugh or do something, look at Wulda and tell her what she had to do and how she had to do it, had to remember that she was there at her side in the kitchen, in the storeroom or the pantry, and it did not seem as if it was as easy for her as before. Wulda had wanted to help her, help Lola, and had told her that if it was about the plants, not to worry so much, because the seedlings would be protected in the kitchen window until spring came again, when Lola could do it, of course, without her help because she would not be in the house, but who knew whether with the help of Katja if she got better or with the help of whoever would come to replace her, could transplant them to the garden like the creeper that had grown up and up much higher than they had thought it would and now was wrapping around the railings up there, and then Lola really laughed and agreed and said something like you are going to be very happy, girl, because you are made for that, for being happy. Wulda wondered if she could be happy, a lot or a little, because Aunt Bauma had assured her that happiness can be achieved only after death when you go to Heaven, and had assured her of this nodding her head at the bed where her mother lay waiting for the sun, breathing so hard that the skin stretched tight around her nose. But her mother had died slowly without complaint, almost content to leave or at least peaceful, without bothering anyone because it was Sunday and Wulda was ironing next to Aunt Bauma, and after that there was more room in the house and she and Aunt Bauma had rearranged the furniture and given the bed with its mattress and pillows and bedclothes to the church, and Aunt Bauma kept saying that happiness could not be found in this world but only in the next one, but now she spoke without looking anywhere, eyes lowered, watching what her fingers were doing with the ball almost dry almost wet that was going to be one of the best molds for hats that could be found in the city. Wulda did not wonder what this other world was or even whether or not she knew, although if someone besides Aunt Bauma spoke about the world for some other reason that was not happiness, in confusion she looked behind all her other thoughts shimmering beyond the curtain of her eyes reaching her neck, forehead, and at times as far from her head as her hands, those two big shiny hulking animals sleeping one wrapped around the other breathing the sweet air of heaven while Lola said they could be the world, why not; but once, intrigued, she had held on to the word happiness and without any possible response had felt a pit, something softer than a pit, a warm cherry between her lips and in that mysterious place where her throat united with her chest where she felt fear, pain, and hunger, but also where, when she discovered that Hans Boher had opened a store on Firen Street and she had begun to go there to buy the broaches and belt loops that Aunt Bauma sent her for, other things happened, as mysterious as the body and death: trembling although it was not cold and singing although she did not know the song and feeling the roughness of the leaves that Lola put between her fingertips to find out what was happening to plants as they grew. However it was not plants that worried Lola, but what did? What made her absent although she was there, as if she were folded, bent double over herself in a way that made it hard to talk or laugh; at times Wulda wondered what it could be, this thing that had attached itself to Lola, had her cornered so she had to fight to get out: a siege, an enclosure, a glass box that she could not see. But she was happy in spite of it all because Lola had not changed like Madame Helena when something worried her, who threw hard chunks of her worry all around like cinders and if they hit someone, so be it. Lola did not. Lola had been made of the clay that Aunt Bauma said the Lord had kneaded in His hands after separating light from darkness and land from water and from the air in the sky, but she herself, Lola herself, when Wulda told her what Aunt Bauma told her, had said that the Lord had put some drops of carissa perfume mixed with the breath of newborn cows and the hundred yellow eyes that float on broth when a fat hen has been boiled for three hours into the clay that His fingers kneaded. Wulda asked if these carissas and hens and cows had existed when the Lord kneaded the clay and Lola laughed at that and said of course: cows, for example, had been the first creatures that the Lord had made. Why, Wulda asked. What a question, really, what a question, Lola answered, well because they are warm and round and take their time chewing and have a map drawn on their tongue and palate, a map of distant lands where palace towers touch the clouds and the kings and queens dress in gold and silver and eat from plates carved from enormous diamonds and emeralds and sleep on mattresses filled with swan down. Wulda had thought a lot about all that and above all about the cows because kings and queens were in books of sacred history, like King David and the Queen of Sheba and not in the world; but since she had never been close to cows, not a single one, although she had seen them from a distance when she passed a dairy with their clattering churns, she had found nothing useful in this line of thought and had accepted what Lola told her. Which usually happened because Lola said things that were true, she had already confirmed that, even things that had not happened yet: she knew they would eventually happen just because Lola had said so. She knew that the carissa and breath of cows and broth were why Lola did not have cinders and Madame Helen did because perhaps the Lord had overdone it when he put them in the clay for making Lola and almost nothing had been left for Madame Helena, and this was why the dumplings that Lola cooked tasted of the countryside and the heavenly air that little animals breathed in a world where there were cows but not kings or queens. It was not as complicated as it seemed. Aunt Bauma had told her that men were all wicked and she had to be very careful and keep away from them because they would make unlucky women unhappy whether they married them or not, and Lola had told her this was true because everyone made an effort to say so and to swear very seriously that this was true, so what she had to do was swear very seriously the opposite, and besides Hans Boher was a good man, a hard and willing worker, tidy, elegant, handsome, and he enjoyed a good job and had said from the beginning that his intentions were serious, that he wanted to marry her and not carry on foolishly, and had repeatedly said she would be very happy with him, and she should not forget what she had told him. Wulda had raised some warm beer to her lips and had promised not to forget it and had wondered what would happen in the house on Scheller Street when she was not there and was Mrs. Boher and she lived opposite Three Republics Park on the other side of the city. She had concluded that nothing would happen, nothing that had not already happened, nothing that Lola had not talked about once, people who come and people who go, people who stay forever, people who get sick or marry and plants that grow and die and are born again and grow. Aunt Bauma had said Wulda was ungrateful because she was leaving the house like that where she had always been treated well and had been given clothing and shoes and gifts for her mother and her home, and this was a sin, so she would have to do penance by returning to Madame Helena's house often to offer to help, but Lola had said just two words when she had told her, as always, what Aunt Bauma said; Lola had stood round like cows, sails unfurled, flags flying high, cannons ready to fire in the middle of the storeroom with her hands on her hips, looked her carefully in the eye, and the mouths of the cannons had fired these two words: that's stupid. Wulda was content. Whatever happened in the house, she would not return: strange women would come who would make you feel paralyzed and dream what you should not, see shadows where they were not, and be afraid of everything, and they would leave and what would remain, nothing, an empty suite that would have to be cleaned and aired out, where rugs would have to be shaken and drawers emptied so threads, a button, pins, and a scrap of silk paper would fall onto the bare floor; curtains taken down that had been impregnated with a perfume that had never been smelled in the house before; picture frames polished, made sooty by the smoke in the fireplace; the bathroom would have to be scrubbed and black hairs cleaned from the drain and the remains of honey soap from the soap dishes and the mirrors polished with an alcohol-soaked cloth; someone would go to the Americas the way Miss Esther was going and who had given her lovely clothes telling her that she would not need them there and promised to send her a post card with a green and yellow parrot perched on the branch of a pineapple tree; someone would go crazy or half-crazy like the General who talked to himself in the corridors and did not seem to see anyone or like Miss Nehala who wore her mother's clothing and sat and called to have her food brought up on trays, and all the others would always be the same like Madame Helena overseeing all of them so seriously, or like the skinny man who looked more like his itty bitty giraffes every day, or the student who looked at her strangely when he looked at her but who had consoled her when her poor mother had died. But the creeper kept growing and one day it would cover the entire wall of the house that faced the garden and it would have to be trimmed so it would not enter the windows and doors. It would not flower because this kind of vine did not have flowers, but its pale green leaves would be bright and pretty, and when Katja recovered and could go out into the garden she would be surprised to see how much it had grown. Wulda would plant a creeper at her house, too, she had already told Hans Boher, and he had promised to dig the hole and put up wires for it to twine on. She would visit Aunt Bauma from time to time, she would, not very often but she would, just as she knew for certain that she would never, ever return to the house on Scheller Street.

28. The Princess

Six square millimeters for each foot
and yet he would certainly need much more space to see it well so
the dark color of the kimono would look right and the hair would
shine when viewed from any direction. It would need a white cloth
like the white silk background that pearls required, as the Japanese
woman in the suite facing the garden had said; silk and satin for
the distant, mute, and almost smiling little lady dressed in mauve
and gold, hair held by little gold pins with pearly heads, a gold
sash that tied in the back with a wide flat bow, and a yellowish
fan that might have once been gold in her raised hand as if to
hide her face, at least the mouth and nose although not those eyes
that revealed a smile. The sweet suffering of those tiny motionless
feet, traversed by two slivers, naughty the smile, savory the taste
of discovery, acrid the dead air in the house where everything was
being sold, furniture, fittings, lamps, utensils, and decorations,
bitter the stale odor of age, of what had been closed up and unused
for a long time, sitting in the cold and dark accumulating white
spots from humidity seeping through the ceiling and the cracks
of carelessly closed doors. He would put her between the dancer
and the monkey, as if they had the duty to entertain her, as if she
were only looking at him after having seen the pirouettes of the
dancer and the bows of the monkey to let him know how much
she had enjoyed the show. The lower shelf, not on the upper shelf

where it might slip and fall and where the fish-man sat who saw everything, knew everything, and was jealous of everything. Wulda approached with the platter: instead of holding it over an open hand within reach and keeping the other hand on the far edge, she desperately held it with two hands, one on each of the longer sides, making it hard to serve himself comfortably. He looked at her angrily but she noticed nothing, only smiled at him briefly, almost a grimace, so different from Kati-Kati's smile; which made him feel sorry for himself and for the effort he had put into erasing or at least muddling the memory by twining it around any other one and closing it tight and hoping it would not arise even disguised in dreams, that fleeting moment when he had lunged forward and the girl, startled or impatient, had fallen back abruptly no doubt pushed by the gaze of the fish-man who had presided over every act that afternoon. It had been an accident, that certainty supported him: an accident. He grasped at the serving utensils, passing one of his hands behind Wulda's arm to bring them nearer but the spoon was too far away, and he sat there tense, frozen, and furious while Madame Helena Lundgren spoke about travel with Miss Esther and was not watching, did not see what was happening: Kati-Kati thought she was important and that was why she had fallen, not because he had attacked. If she had stood still, nothing would have happened, but the fish-man had been behind it all, a force of destiny behind her wavering body, useless hands, horrified eyes, and the fall, and then Wulda herself was running her fingers over the edge of the platter to give him more room to lift up the serving utensils and finally he could put some meat and vegetables on his plate. The fish-man staring through the water, an open door, the steps of Kati-Kati coming down the staircase: it had all pushed him to leave his room and once past the door to congratulate himself because only the two of them were in the corridor; the girl came down the last steps, he waited below, she jumped to get away, he reached for her, she moved fast, hesitating, and falling back, her head hitting the edge of the steps she had just come down without even enough time to cry out, he returned to his room and stared at the eyes of the fish-man for hours until it had grown so dark he had to turn on the lights and only then did he hear voices and hurried steps although the doctor had come much later, even after the evening meal, which had been the first meal disastrously served by Wulda. The girl would recover, how could she not, please, it had been such an insignificant fall, not a fatal accident like the one involving the boy from the house across the street months previous run over by a coach and trampled by horses; no, this was nothing, just a stumble, a fall, a contusion, nothing, she would of course heal, absolutely, but if she healed he would have to flee, to escape Kati-Kati's eyes which would open and search him out and say: it was him. Unless she had forgotten everything, which according to what he had read somewhere might happen since sometimes people who suffer a blow to the head and lose consciousness later awake having lost their memory, not knowing who they are or where they are or what has happened to them; he would need to leave. He would take only the little Japanese princess wrapped in silk so she would not suffer, soft and warm in the hollow of his hand, no other treasure, just her, and by no means the fish-man with his fish-man eyes capable of slithering over rocks and walls. He would leave his treasures behind and he would not care because she would go with him, her porcelain soul, silken heart, pearls on the pins of her headdress, and secret eyes of black amber, to wherever the wind and sea would take them. He did not know exactly when Wulda had taken away his plate or exactly when she had poured more wine in his glass: when Kati-Kati returned to serve dinner, he would not be in the house, he would not eat creamy sauces or well-seasoned meat, he would not chew nuts like bits of butter nor would his tongue help wine slip past his palate and down his throat, he would not hear that Lundgren woman's voice, or see daylight appear through the window of his rooms before everyone else. With all his strength he wanted to twist the day, unite the flavors, set aside time, forget all those people who again and again sat at that table to look for words in the folds of their more than imperfect memories and throw them at each other and smile, above all the women, even this poor-spirited girl who served them; to smile in the desert where there was no one and nothing, not even a wolf whose teeth shone as it tried to bite a mouthful it would never reach. A china and silk princess, with slivers in her feet, natural hair sold by some woman, threaded into her head lock by lock and arranged with a nest of pearl-headed gilt pins from a country of fans and domes and bells, he would take her and leave, and with that would suppress the footsteps on the stairs, the gaze of the fish-man from the upper shelf as if from the sea, the voice of Helena Lundgren giving an order that no one could dispute, and the Japanese woman entering as portent for this other woman, herald of the truer one of flesh, blood, and saliva, in the house on Scheller Street.

29. Forever

The word forever did not have a special meaning after it had been said and thought through, contemplated like an object or mechanism, like something concrete outside of herself; on the contrary, now it meant nothing, deprived of width, a mere line of meager letters, something secretive or medicinal you placed in your mouth, this word briefly chosen to avoid all betrayal, another to seek improbable consolation: she had resorted to that word like a refuge and closed a door behind herself after finally locating the room filled with distrust and every kind of suspicion and objection, windowless, airless, suffocating, and maternal, like the divan for an over-protected sick woman. She said: I am leaving forever, but she had not said that to anyone and even the excitement of saying it had become self-delusion, a string of letters that had lost their sound and meaning along with their noise and weight, and she did not hear them, they only seemed to be a hint of music, a brief upward trill of a flute when night had fallen, not in a concert but solo, improvised, coming from an upper floor from time to time; above all in the morning seeing someone pass the curtainless glass in the windows, the somber tones of an oboe, a string vibrating with some fickle note cut off as if the bow or hand had given up on it forever, forever and ever. It had been the last lunch forever and ever in the house and it had not been much different from earlier ones; she had conversed with Madame Helena, they had said a few things like oh but is it as far away as Japan, do you remember Madame Nashiru? and they had said the distances are unimaginable for those of us who are older although of course not in Japan where everything is so very small and close unlike the Americas that await you, and finally they had said do not fail to write us and remember us, won't you? But after lunch, waiting or watching the minutes pass that at some point would become hours in this world that no longer existed for her and which she could no longer touch or brighten, the two open suitcases on the bed, telling herself that all that remained was to put what she needed from her boudoir into her handbag. Time tried to overcome her and hurt her, talcum, comb, powder, to make her weep or lament the now naked walls in the room, tweezers, nail clipper, toothbrush, the drawers smelled of lavender and above all the tea shop that had been a fragment of her life, hand towel, bar of soap, nail file, a long waylay in the presence of noisy gentlemen and solid women who with a toss of their head said yes or no and accepted each other so easily, sensibly, over a cup of French chocolate in winter with their coats over the curved backs of chairs, rose water, lanolin, lipstick, as if it had been a fragment of floral life by Felix Ziem, "maître de la lumière et des couleurs vibrantes" which she could never cut out from her memories about the wall in the second-floor corridor of the house on Scheller Street which she was going to leave forever, forever and ever, or the flowers behind the green leather-topped desk in a corner of the salon in "Miraflora" where Mr. Celsus had suggested not going away alone and hidden like her name, so distant on the misty far side of the world, unknown and mute in a language she would not understand and where no one would understand hers, where great rivers, giant trees, and vast plains confounded the measure of all things, sizable letters taken like medicine and now meaning nothing or they do but they do not know what, only a broken string, the sound of the violin d'amore, the light of other stars all along the journey. The drop that never falls from the spigot, the flame that never dies on the wood, the bluish steam at the spout of the teapot, the grille on the window when the day breaks outside, the first step toward the gangway of the ship, they are also a fraction of an entire lifetime and little things done without thinking, details of a painting like the color of a vase in which autumn flowers wilt before a summer landscape that has already been left behind, a single instant of existence that smells like the black ink of the notes in a musical staff, the music of wisdom interrupting words and closing mouths, the black smell of wick wafting up on a candlelit night. She thought it was like death to leave "Miraflora" in other hands no matter how efficient they were, to shut the suitcases, to cross the gangway genuinely alone, to forget the other things that she now no longer remembered whether they belonged to her or not, if they were things she had carefully done to avoid dying or things like the rest of them that had filled the space of a second, the space where she had decided her life. She left behind all the time she had built, all the music in one note, all the feelings in all the words in a single word, a sleeping girl, a window opening onto the garden, another window she had never looked out of, an atrocious moment when she had closed her eyes as some horses bolted past. She had briefly bid farewell to Mr. Celsus and would not say farewell to anyone in the boarding house, to no one except for Madame Helena who in her role as lady of the house was going to be at the door to say good-bye: she would travel across the round belly of the world and this is what made her feel that she would return somewhere, that she was not leaving forever. Perhaps she would always return to the psalm-like sounds in the first song, the vibration in the ear like a drumhead beaten by clay-colored hands, she would return to the heart, the black smell of black ink impregnating the night and staining the fingers of the father she left behind, the inconclusive memories drawn on maps in her childhood room, other faces and other names, her own name hidden among the flowers garlanding the wall in the instant that it took to leave anyplace in the world for someplace else that would never again be the house on Scheller Street.

30. Exaltation

What more intense satisfaction could he expect than her absence when nothing had been said? White china felt smooth to the touch and sparkled for the eyes in the dining room lights during the moment when young Gangulf tried to convince himself that he had triumphed; eyes on the bright china, the white voice of the cups against saucers, the creamer next to the bottle of milk, the faint silver cry of the cutlery that burned his skin as if he had lain naked in the sun for the ages since the beginning of time under the gaze of visionaries, pushing him toward the clarity of bonfires, sparks, the reverberation of genius; everything left him blind, groping, trembling, becoming his own prophet in search of the conquerors' pride. He took another step toward the stairway thinking he would manage to climb to the second floor and stalk to the door of the room at the end, a hidden and well-known door, his steps as light as a fox whose reddish color blends in with fallen leaves, light as someone walking suspiciously in a strange city, like the goshawk, like a sloop, light as the vole and the sun-dew, like venal sin, he who sought destiny in sacrifice; but in the end he paused at the foot of the stairway, turned, and entered the salon, crossed it, and came to the dining room whose doors were always open at that hour, dressed in metal and brilliant silvery lights that he almost never looked at. If nothing had been said, what did absence mean? He allowed himself to greet everyone, to sit at the table with its ivory tablecloth white china white flowers that he could not identify with yellow spots in their center, to ponder an apprenticeship that would raise him up to what he called exaltation even when that word very rarely appeared in his ruminations: it lived in truth rather than in hushed pronunciation, or no, like the sensation of acid fire, like illness or the inferno and possibly even the flight of angels to the foot of a throne of an indifferent god, cruel at times and incapable of meting out punishment in a show of deformed justice; a feeling of safety inside that became heavy and ignorant, too clumsy to know what was truly happening to him but alert to an urgent desire. Although he answered Mr. Pallud, he quickly looked at the General: here we have, he said to himself, a miserable man, and he knew unhappiness at that moment, avid for a pain that would authorize him to go up to the second floor, to knock on the door of Miss Esther's room and enter smiling, to wish her a good trip, to surprise her, disturb her, finally to leave forgetting that absence can offer itself as the pretext of satisfaction, to go to his room where he would suffer this unnamed pain that was not his, as distant from him as a far-off land where he mistakenly went time and again. This woman, sharp and soft and smooth and keen as a dagger, dangerous to herself in her beautiful absolute determination, daughter of the Nibelheim Cave gods, would dream about him, speak to him, follow him, embark with him in the ship that would fight in all the rivers of the world for his fortune against the current flowing to the sea: he would make that happen without the disguise of terror, without a cry, without confession, without having said anything. Young, fatuous, miserly, far from his home and parents, the student thought that if treachery killed his determination he would wind up like that, like that pale watery-eyed old man who spent his time visiting second-hand shops in search of the dolls he adored and perhaps revered, worshiping ridiculously, naked or on his knees or flagellating himself or talking

to them as if they were his children or dreaming that they grew and
grew until they devoured him, always gray, quietly saying you have
to see this treasure, just imagine, it is described there in the third
volume of Heindesberg in a footnote in the chapter which studies
national figurines what a find is it possible that these people did not
know what they had this happens from a lack of information and
most of all from a lack of interest. Under the spell of the growing
fire that burned in the ashen man's eyes, he told himself perhaps
no or perhaps yes he would call it a destiny like the General's and
toward which little by little his mouth had been twisting the way
the openings of his jacket pockets yawned at him and his gaze
lowered until it was dragging on the floor unable to move his lids or
pupils, his two eyes turned into hard agates left unpolished on the
banks of a solitary and sluggish river. He finished his tea and said
yes, of course he would be delighted to see the figurine and indeed
it seemed very strange that Mr. Pallud had found it, so exquisite,
exactly six months after Madame Nashiru had left the house on
Scheller Street.

31. The Women of the House on Scheller Street

Awaiting the last breath of summer, the first puff of autumn, Madame Helena ordered the front door left ajar and the chancel door locked once tea had been served in the house on Scheller Street. Because a coach had been requested at six on the dot and because without a doubt the doctor would come to see Katja as he had promised the day before, that day the door to the street would remain open although the chancel door was closed as always. Anxiety could be seen gathering like fog in every corner and angle where walls met, visible to anyone who noticed the shaking lights, who listened to the whispers of women who had lived part of their lives in those rooms, men clearing their throats as they counted their accumulated money not really over something bothersome in their throats but due to a kind of invincible spiritual unease that awoke each time strong hands and weak will undertook that sordid duty. But Katja slept in a poor imitation of the sleep of nubile girls, slept as far from Scheller Street as possible, so disconnected to life that she seemed to see Wulda at dawn, and if Katja did not see her, then who, what other woman could have guessed the little frights that afflicted injured women and disenchanted men who had once lived there and returned to those rooms to sigh, fear, resist, and delay when death drew near. Only Katja knew these things; not Lola who was always so immersed in life that she accepted whatever came, shouldered it and stripped it of all pain and mystery; had she seen the agitation in the house, Lola would have opened all the windows to let the wind enter, or would have embraced the pale shadowy women and fed their men something that would have let them rest without need of Mass or psalms; not Wulda, who only looked at Katja when she was not anticipating her happiness in this world alongside Hans Boher and wishing that the eyelids of this sleeping girl were transparent so she could see her thoughts and soothe her with the words that surely she was awaiting in her sleep. Wulda stayed at night and Aunt Bauma thought it was proper to offer abnegation to the Virgin but not be absent at dawn for housecleaning before going to work; Wulda sat on the empty bed beside Katja and watched her, dozed a bit, got up to count her breaths, closed her eyes, slept, woke, leaned over the ill woman's chest and tried to hear her heart as she had seen the doctor do, lay down again and slept again and got up again until the sun rose and she went to the kitchen to make Lola's breakfast, the first meal of the house. Wulda did not mind being beside her, in fact she looked forward to it, sure that Katja would be brought back to life with the warmth of her body, would talk, would tell her something, would finally ask for something.

Silence was prolonged that day beyond tea time: Madame Helena had entered the empty dining room late and the General had just left, and then she had shut herself in her office on the lower floor. She was there when the coach arrived for Miss Esther. The coachman knocked, waited, and knocked again, and Madame Helena opened her door at the moment when Wulda was almost running toward the chancel door. Madame Helena gave her a severe look: nothing abrupt, no running, shouting or even strident laughter, that was the first thing she instructed those who came to work in her house. Wulda, oblivious to all this, opened the door, asked the coachman to wait, and came back. Madame Helena told her not so fast, please, the house wasn't on fire and the river wasn't flooding, go notify Miss Esther that the coach had arrived and come down carrying her suitcase. The women of the house on Scheller Street, sitting on the stairway, leaning on the walls, a petalless flower in hand, looking from the windows, closing parasols, deploring that another one of them was leaving, going so far, suffering so much, and with so many hopes to forget, and one of them remembered the moment when she had left through that same door never to return in life, but Madame Helena, very upright and calm, was the only one who had returned in life; she only thought that it was a difficult afternoon with Miss Esther's departure, the doctor's visit, the answer that she was awaiting from Mr. Ruprecht to whom she had sent word that the suite was available, and perhaps the arrival of the new maid who had promised to be there at eight although with staff whom you have not personally trained you can never be sure of anything. She had made life suit her tastes, she had organized time into a serenity that made her feel proud and essential: without her, what would have become of the house on Scheller Street? A tangle of problems, constant disarray, insolent servants, disastrous hours, disorderly people, untidiness and even uncleanliness everywhere. Or it would be an abandoned ruin. Or the house of a family like every other with problems, arguments, anger, and even tragedies like that boy she herself had seen die beneath the hoofs of the bolting horses due to the irresponsibility of a mother who had let him play in the street so late. The women who had left the house on Scheller Street wept in silence for their dead children and dried their tears when Miss Esther and Wulda came down the stairway. There was a quick farewell full of smiles and good wishes, a peremptory good-bye and hardly a murmur, and that would have been the end of it except that Wulda had turned back to the house after carrying the suitcase to the coachman at the moment when Miss Esther left: they met face to face, and Madame Helena, who had shaken the traveler's hand, watched with surprise as Miss Esther put her hands on Wulda's shoulders, brought her face close, and kissed her on the cheek. Miss Esther got into the coach, and it left. Wulda turned with a dance step, held herself tight tight tight as if she were cold and felt in one blow all the happiness that she was going to have in this world with Hans Boher. Madame Helena looked displeased. The women who had lived there told each other that it had been worthwhile to answer that warm call like returning to the nest and see the afternoon die at the house on Scheller Street.

32. Medical Science

Night took possession of Scheller Street, and Novalis, baleful and melancholic, passed again like a shadow through Katja's dreams, in her sleep awaiting the lips of Julia the Savior. Facing the fire, Lola feels Katja's torpor place itself between her and the world: but what does it matter, dinner is ready and served on platters that Wulda is taking upstairs almost nimbly, almost floating as if she were now accustomed to the task that she was not going to have to do anymore because Madame Helena had spoken with the new servant in her office, a strapping girl with red hair and full lips who came recommended by Madame Hartenbach. Lola, annoyed and tired, or as she tells herself discouraged and exhausted, sits at the table in the kitchen storeroom waiting for Wulda while, in the checkerboard of the sky, Aristarchus of Samos enjoys plotting the new design for the constellations. Lola does not care if Wulda is late, perhaps Madame Helena has called her in, perhaps she has had some problem with the platters, all she wants to do is sit still like a stone so that nothing happens, so that death does not come to take her along with Katja because she is suddenly sure that Katja is going to die; she has a thick bitter taste in her mouth that has risen up like a silent invader from her stomach and she thinks she is also going to die, that death is going to come disguised as a pilgrim or civil servant dressed in black with a big hooked nose and ravenous little eyes and is going to look at them, at her and Katja, look at them hard, ponder whether to take them or not, and in the end is going to decide yes and gesture for them to follow and they will have no choice but to obey, and then she feels a pain sharper than all the pain in the world and she breaks in two holding her belly in her hands.

Impatient but trying not to show it, Madame Helena asked Herta the Red questions while the women of the house on Scheller Street milled around her, touched her hair the color of dying fire, sniffed her, and checked under her arms, down her neckline, between her legs, and behind her ears. Herta's eyelids were fine and dark and had visible blue veins when the girl blinked. Madame Helena was telling her that for the time being she would have to sleep in an improvised bedroom because there was a sick girl, a convalescent girl she corrected herself, in the servant's room. The rich and slender women, women in pink and gold who had lived in the house on Scheller Street, covered their mouths to roar with laughter so the public would not consider them impolite coarse country girls like the one in dormition whom death was going to take before dawn. Oh, Luduv, Katja sighed, don't leave me alone, and Luduv got up and Novalis's arm could be seen at the far end of the street where a coach pulled by bolting horses appeared every night to run past and disappear in a gray cloud of clay kneaded by the Lord's hands under Aunt Bauma's attentive gaze. Mr. Pallud entered the brightly lit salon and seeing that he was alone, left, paused in the corridor at the foot of the stairs looking at the place where Katja had fallen face-up against the edge of the steps and thought that he should go see her, thought that he would want to be there when Kati-Kati opened her eyes, thought that perhaps she would never open them again, and then returned to the salon at the moment when someone knocked on the door. Mr. Pallud remained in the salon, merely listening, not leaving, not moving, and heard the door being opened, heard the doctor's voice, another door, the voice of Madame Helena, of the girl who served dinner, and another voice of a woman he did not know: if the fish-man devoured the princess, what would become of him? He would go back, he decided, he would go back to his room immediately and wait there for the commotion of doctors and strange women to be over. In the corridor he passed the doctor and Madame Helena, and they all said good evening, but he saw no one else.

Medical science worries about what is lost: sleep, appetite, composure, blood, or strength; it attempts to recover them and when it cannot, to replace them; it touches bodies, probes them, searches them, opens them and sews them up, both holy and profane, infinitely wise, infinitely ignorant, using only two weapons, desire and rejection, always defeated by death, always defeating death. With two fingers, the doctor very gently opened one of Katja's eyes. The women whimpered but he did not hear them, studying what he saw in the eye. He lowered the eyelid with his fingers, carefully again, and palpitated the sleeping girl's head. Luduv! Katja said because she had seen him come in through the window, and he smiled at her. The doctor said there was little hope that Katja would ever wake up, to wait twenty-four hours more and if the situation had not changed, he would recommend taking her to Mercy Hospital. He left the room with Madame Helena after having wiped his hand on a white kerchief moistened with alcohol, and behind the door that Madame Helena closed, the women of the house, laughing, welcomed Luduv, and Katja sat up to hug him. In the corridor on the first floor Madame Helena and the doctor encountered young Gangulf who accompanied them downstairs. At that moment and as Wulda went ahead to open the chancel door, a sharp howl exploded in the house, a long desperate shriek like an animal snapped by a steel-toothed trap it had not seen. The house stopped, the air went still, breaths ceased, the party in Katja's room jumped out the window in a flight of gauze and braids and satin slippers and Luduv's floating hair, Katja's eyes shining, mouths full of laughter, and it was lost in the sweet air of the heavens where Novalis's blue flowers opened. Madame Helena and the doctor looked at each other and only Wulda moved and ran down the stairs toward the kitchen. When the doctor arrived, he saw Lola's head resting on Wulda's lap, who was stroking her forehead. Lola, enormous as the world's oldest mountains, dress stained with blood, and smiling, lifted up her hands looking for something to grab before another tense pain came. She knows what this is, finally she knows, and when the sorrow for Katja disappears she begins to look around as if he were there with her, the man with the gold teeth who pursues her and surrounds her and corners her on the top floor of the tavern next to the river.

Much can be said of medical science but not that it wastes an opportunity when desire is bellowing and the lady of death has left, satiated. The doctor took off his jacket, rolled up his sleeves, and fell to his knees next to Lola:

"You, girl," he said to Wulda, "get behind her and hold her hands, and you, madame," he said to Madame Helena, "open my case, give me those scissors, that's it, that white cloth, the forceps, and look for towels to take the baby."

Miss Esther, rocked to sleep by the train, dreamed that the next day she would walk on the deck of a ship; Mr. Pallud paced impatiently in the corridor; young Gangulf also thought about ships; for the first time other hands closed the doors of "Miraflora" while the General felt death brush past him and move on this time and this time only; and Miss Nehala Simeoni tried to get up from her armchair to go to the door to see if the servant was coming with the dinner tray. In London, in the boarding house of Mrs. Stewart, Madame Nashiru took clothing from her suitcases and placed them in the wardrobes while in the dining room Mrs. Stewart told her guests that the woman she had just introduced came from Tokyo to open a jewelry store in London that would sell pearls, especially pearls, pearls from Saboga, Niushu, and the warm seas of Siganda. Madame Helena climbed the stairs laboriously, heavily, which she had gone down with such composure and decision every morning before the clock in the salon struck eight: she hoped that Herta could serve dinner with decorum, hoped the night would pass soon, that another day would arrive, that Wulda would leave, that Katja would get well, that Mr. Ruprecht would come and occupy the suite on the ground floor that opened to the garden, that everything would be the same as before, tranquil, quiet, restrained, and unchanging for a long time. The house creaked in the night, and the women's laughter echoed all along Mill Alley, on the water in the river, in the treetops, on the balconies, a small round thought like a cherry warmed by the sun on the facade of the house on Scheller Street.

About the Author

Angélica Gorodischer, daughter of the writer Angélica de Arcal, was born in 1929 in Buenos Aires and has lived most of her life in Rosario, Argentina. Her more than twenty books include *Kalpa Imperial*, *Trafalgar*, and *Tumba de jaguares*. She has received many awards for her work, including most recently a Konex Special Mention Award.

About the Translator

Born in Wisconsin, Sue Burke moved to Madrid, Spain, in 1999. Her fiction and poetry have appeared in many magazines and anthologies. She has worked as a journalist and editor and is a member of the American Translators Association and the Asociación Española de Fantasía, Ciencia Ficción, y Terror.

When you run into Trafalgar Medrano at the Burgundy or the Jockey Club and he tells you about his latest intergalactic sales trip, don't try to rush him. He likes to stretch things out over seven double coffees. No one knows whether he actually travels to the stars, but he's the best storyteller around, so why doubt him?

"Perhaps the strangest thing about these tales is how easily one forgets the mechanics of their telling. Medrano's audiences are at first reluctant to be taken in by yet another digressive, implausible monologue about sales and seductions in space. But soon enough, they are urging the teller to get on with it and reveal what happens next. The discerning reader will doubtless agree."—*Review of Contemporary Fiction*

paper · $16 · 9781618730329 | ebook · 9781618730336

ANGÉLICA GORODISCHER

Translated by Ursula K. Le Guin

KALPA IMPERIAL

the greatest empire that never was

Multiple storytellers weave oral histories, fairy tales, and political commentaries into the story of a fabled nameless empire which has risen and fallen innumerable times. Beggars become emperors, democracies become dictatorships, history becomes legends and stories.

"The history of an imaginary empire in a series of tales that adopt the voice of a marketplace storyteller. . . . While the point of each tale eludes paraphrase, the cumulative burden is the imperfectibility of human society . . . Le Guin's translation, which ranges from blunt to elegant to oracular, seems like the ideal medium for this grim if inescapable message."— *New York Times Book Review* Summer Reading Pick

paper · $16 · 9781931520058 | ebook · 9781618730190